remember me

estelle laure

WEDNESDAY BOOKS
NEW YORK

First published in the United States by Wednesday Books, an imprint of St. Martin's Publishing Group

REMEMBER ME. Copyright © 2022 by Estelle Laure. All rights reserved. Printed in the United States of America. For information, address St. Martin's Publishing Group, 120 Broadway, New York, NY 10271.

www.wednesdaybooks.com

Designed by Michelle McMillian

Library of Congress Cataloging-in-Publication Data

Names: Laure, Estelle, author.
Title: Remember me / Estelle Laure.
Description: First edition. | New York : Wednesday Books, an imprint of
    St. Martin's Publishing Group, 2022. | Audience: Ages 13-18.
Identifiers: LCCN 2021016070 | ISBN 9781250261939 (hardcover) |
    ISBN 9781250261946 (ebook)
Subjects: LCSH: Memory—Juvenile fiction. | Amnesia—Juvenile fiction. |
    Recovered memory—Juvenile fiction. | Grief—Juvenile fiction. |
    Identity (Psychology)—Juvenile fiction. | Mothers and daughters—
    Juvenile fiction. | Human experimentation in medicine—Juvenile fiction. |
    Young adult fiction. | CYAC: Memory—Fiction. | Amnesia—Fiction. |
    Grief—Fiction. | Identity—Fiction. | Mothers and daughters—Fiction. |
    Human experimentation in medicine—Fiction. | LCGFT: Psychological fiction.
Classification: LCC PZ7.1.L38 Re 2021 | DDC 813.6 [Fic]—dc23
LC record available at https://lccn.loc.gov/2021016070

Our books may be purchased in bulk for promotional, educational, or business use. Please contact your local bookseller or the Macmillan Corporate and Premium Sales Department at 1-800-221-7945, extension 5442, or by email at MacmillanSpecialMarkets@macmillan.com.

First Edition: 2022

10 9 8 7 6 5 4 3 2 1

For Sara Goodman, supreme eater of stars

But to feel nothing so you don't have to
feel anything—what a waste.

—ANDRÉ ACIMAN, *Call Me by Your Name*

Now that my ladder's gone
I must lie down where all the ladders start
In the foul rag and bone shop of the heart.

—WILLIAM BUTLER YEATS, "The Circus Animals' Desertion"

one

*Wouldn't you like to forget every bad thing
that ever happened to you?
Forget that dog that died when you were six, the one who
stole your heart; Forget the girl who rejected you, the father
who abandoned you, the mother who beat you, the boy who
dumped you on prom night.
Forget everything that no longer serves you.
Be a virgin again; An innocent who has not known tragedy
or betrayal by others or more importantly betrayal perpetrated
by the self; Be who you were meant to be: whole, untainted,
and mostly and best of all, Be pain-free.*

—Dr. Vargas, founder of Tabula Rasa, Inc.
The Rally to Save the Youth, Angel Wing Bridge (2031)

Memories of the last time I saw my mother slip through my mind like water over river rocks.

I ask myself:

Did I kiss her goodbye that morning as she and Dad hurried out the door to go skiing? I feel her lips against my cheek, smell toothpaste and her orange blossom lotion. Then just as fast as that memory comes in I can see her rushing for the keys calling out a quick goodbye as I stared at my phone, not coming over to me at all, never even approaching.

Did I imagine she gave me a last, longing look or that she took an extra beat to blow me a kiss, or that the instant the door clicked shut behind her I wanted to run to her and tell her not to go? Am I adding in my sense of foreboding—some premonitory lurch as the car started up outside—so I can feel a little better about what came after?

I give myself a little slap on the cheek.

I'm not imagining *all* the strange things that have happened this morning.

After all, someone *has* left me a secret message and I have the piece of paper in my hand to prove it.

I have not made it up.

I'm sitting on my dad's old Chevy truck at my faux adobe apartment complex next to the sign that reads 838 Tierra Pointe Villas. I'm pretty sure it was a nice place when Gran and Pop-pop moved into it right after 9/11, but thirty years later it's a slowly crumbling clump of dirt.

I have the keys to Dad's Chevy in my bag, tied onto a piece of leather, but I'm here waiting for Turtle because I don't drive it.

I know that. I just don't know why.

I'm holding the piece of paper between my fingers. I raise it up to the light and check for invisible ink or pen imprints, evidence of another page in the notebook it was ripped from, but the space around the words is smooth and white.

MEET ME ON THE LITTLE BLUE BUS
7:45 5/19/32

It's now 7:45 on May the eighteenth of the year 2032.

The sun is a gold Frisbee bobbing on a clear lake, and my block is serene and uncomplicated with its rows of two-story structures. It's too early in the day for parties or fights or for couples kissing against streetlights, and Turtle is late as usual. Everything is normal and yet it is not.

I don't know of a little blue bus so I type LITTLE BLUE BUS, OWL NOOK, NM into my phone and when the search turns up a whole bunch of things including over six thousand customer review ratings, my breath freezes in my throat.

Apparently the bus runs from this part of Old Town up to the ski valley thirty minutes away. It's free and makes four stops hourly when the valley is open and twice a day off-season, once at 7:45 a.m. and once at 5:15 p.m. There's a map and a picture of a friendly looking Chicano man with his hand up in a wave and a sentence in bold about how tips are appreciated. There's also a picture of the bus, which is bigger than a minivan and smaller than a city bus and has a bright yellow Zia on it. LITTLE BLUE BUS, it reads across the side, in colors that match the symbol.

It's real. It exists. And yet it can't.

I slide my phone into my jacket pocket, but it's not smooth. My hands shake. I have lived in Owl Nook, New Mexico, my entire life. It is impossible there should be this bus driving through town and I do not know about it. I used to live in a subdivision like Turtle and now I live in an apartment complex ten blocks away, which could account for me not knowing about it back then, but still. *Still.* I've lived here with Gran for almost a year and I pride myself on knowing everything there is to know about this place. I should definitely know that there's a bus that shuttles to Owl Nook Ski Valley and back every hour.

I must know it. And yet I don't.

It doesn't make sense.

Nothing is making much sense.

First I woke up with a headache so bad I felt compelled to make sure there wasn't an ax lodged in my skull. I took some ibuprofen, brushed my teeth, and got dressed, I guess. I don't remember that part but I'm in a pair of suit pants, a button-down shirt, and my spring jacket, not currently naked so I must have put on clothes at some point.

Things were already considerably odd, and then when I was getting my jewelry on, reaching for my second earring, I found this piece of paper in my closet.

A note.

A clue tucked carefully under my jewelry box, sticking out from the bottom just enough that I could see it. My feet felt fuzzy as kittens and spots spattered across my field of vision. I woke up a little while later staring at the ceiling with the back of my head throbbing like a sore tooth. At least the location of my headache had changed from front to back. Silver linings. When I was little I always thought fainting was super romantic, but this felt awful. I let myself lie there a minute, then Gran called me into the kitchen for breakfast, pausing her diatribe at the radio long enough to yell my name, then went back to swearing. I got up, went in, had some toast with strawberry jam, and now here we are.

I'm not certain how my backpack wound up slung over my shoulder, or even how I got out to this curb where I usually meet my friends in the mornings. I don't remember saying goodbye to Gran or putting on a jacket or walking down the second-floor stairs. I'm just . . . here.

MEET ME ON THE LITTLE BLUE BUS
7:45 5/19/32

No matter how many times I look at the note, I don't magically recognize the handwriting. It's not Turtle's curvy cursive or Jack's blockish scrawl and yet it fills me with dread and excitement, my whole body jittering like my eyes recognize something my brain can't. It's a maddening itch just out of reach.

I hear the music and rumble of Turtle's old Jeep before she even turns the corner.

I hop off the truck and pull on my backpack.

It's heavy. Unusually heavy.

I unzip it and find four bottles of orange juice standing next to each other, all full and cold. I must have been really out of it this morning because I don't remember putting those in there and why would I? I pull out three of the bottles and put them in the truck as Turtle slides up to the curb. She lets her sunglasses slip down her nose so she's looking at me over the white rims.

"Morning, earthling!" she says, turning down her stereo just enough that she can carry on a conversation. She's in a semi-boho dress with little purple flowers on it and some chunky necklace hanging over her bosom that probably belonged to her great-great-grandmother or something. Turtle never wears anything new. She's a chronic recycler, upcycler, and repurposer. As soon as I see her I start to feel a little less separate from everything. The world comes into focus and I don't feel so much like I'm underwater.

Jack, Turtle's partner, gets out and pulls the lever on the seat so it folds forward, then lets me climb in the back. They have a tweed jacket on with a pink handkerchief tucked into the front pocket and they give me a little bow before clicking the seat back into place. There's not a person on this earth who wouldn't think Jack was beautiful. There's something about them that's so completely self-assured people drop to their knees and worship them wherever they go. They're made even more attractive by their absolute devotion to Turtle. The world watches Jack and Jack watches Turtle. That's just the way it is.

"Why so sullen, friend?" Jack asks.

"I'm not sullen," I say, mustering a smile. "Just quiet. I can be quiet, can't I?"

"Rarely," Jack says. "And your fake smile sucks."

"It's either that or RBF."

"RBF," Jack says. "Always."

"It's been a weird morning." I reach into my pocket and feel the paper between my fingers. "That's all."

Jack and Turtle look at each other. Jack arches their eyebrows meaningfully. I don't catch the meaning, except to know the dynamics between us have shifted. When we were younger, it was Turtle and me, then as of two years ago it was Turtle and me and Jack, and now it's Turtle and Jack and sometimes me. Plus, all of Jack's friends took over and gave Turtle a whole other community I'm only partially involved with. I'm not super bitter about it. They're in love and Turtle is finding herself. It's fair.

I've never had a boyfriend so I don't know what that kind of love is like, what it would be to want to fall into someone else's face.

Wait.

I've never had a boyfriend.

Is that right?

It doesn't feel right.

It doesn't feel *true*.

Whatever Turtle and Jack are communicating via eyebrows starts out being about me, but then both their expressions soften. This is when soul music should come on the radio. Everything slows down and they gaze at each other while the Jeep rattles crankily and I sit in the back trying to look anywhere except at them. Turtle strokes the side of Jack's cheek. It's so *intimate*, but I think we've all had enough of me telling them to get a room. As annoyed as I used to get, I've learned to deal.

When they're done mooning at each other, Jack turns around while Turtle adjusts her lip gloss in the rearview mirror.

"You get any perkier, I'm going to get you some pom-poms

and force you into cheerleader servitude until you turn that frown upside down," Jack says to me. "Why so glum?"

"Excuse you." Turtle turns her attention back to the road as she throws the Jeep into drive. "I'll thank you not to disrespect the cheerleaders. They work hard. You clearly have no idea the amount of discipline required." Turtle flicks her hair over her shoulder. "The only reason I am not one is that I don't have an adequate level of school spirit or interest in sports and I don't like to show my legs. Cheerleading is just not my frequency."

Jack and I grin at each other. Turtle got ahold of some "live your best life" type class on the AHA MOMENT NETWORK™, and now she's always talking about frequencies and whether or not people and/or things are in hers. Saying something is not in your frequency seems to me like a way of saying you hate it.

"You have nice legs," Jack offers, tapping on the side door. Jack is a *killer* drummer and can't keep their hands from drumming all the time, even when there's no music. It's fun to watch.

"Thanks, honey," Turtle says. "But I didn't say I don't have nice legs. I'm fully aware that I got my maternal great-great grandmother Ethel's legs, which are clearly superior. I said I don't like to show them. Plus, I like a flowy silhouette, which is why I've chosen the red twirly thing for the ceremony."

Only another week until graduation and then we'll never be the three of us going to school in this car again. They're leaving in August. Turtle got into Columbia and Jack is going to Sarah Lawrence so it's to New York for both of them, which feels like it might as well be Mars from here.

I'm going to stay to finish high school and then I don't know what. I used to travel with my parents so they could ski all over the place: Japan, British Columbia, all different states, Switzerland. I never found anywhere I like as much as Owl Nook. Nowhere else feels like it could be home. I'm here, forever probably, and Turtle and Jack will move on and I'll have to make it through my senior year alone. This is the suck of having your only real friends one year ahead of you in school. Damn Turtle and her grade-skipping.

Turtle reaches into the bag she has resting between her legs and pops a Taki in her mouth. "I don't prefer jumping. Or actually, my tits don't prefer jumping."

Jack snorts.

"You be a 36E and talk to me about it." Turtle adjusts herself. "I wasn't made for flips and jaunty optimistic leaping."

"Acknowledged. Anyway, that's not the point," Jack says, handing me a coffee. Reusable container of course. "The point is Blue's in a mood."

"Indeed she is," Turtle says, raising one eyebrow. "I have the perfect solution, for no mood can withstand the power of this song, no human is strong enough to resist its pull, least of all our little girl Blue."

She turns up the soundtrack from the classic movie *Moulin Rouge*, which is admittedly my Achilles' heel. No amount of headachy weirdness can keep me from absolutely crowing the "Elephant Love Medley" at the top of my lungs. Everything drifts off into the wind along with our voices.

"Maybe if Blue was in show choir she'd have to make out with Kevin instead of you." Jack knows good and well I'm not joining show choir. I can only imagine what it would be like to dance and sing at the same time. Not good or fun, at least not when executed by me. I am always tripping over my own feet, falling down, bumping into walls. I can totally waggle my limbs and lose myself in a dance, but choreography is a hard no.

Anyway, Kevin Orozco, one of Jack's friends, has been tasked with laying a fat kiss on Turtle at the end of the performance they're doing as the opener for the graduation ceremony next week and is so far doing a very poor job. He told Turtle his penis inverts when he thinks about kissing girls.

"It's not making out," Turtle says. "It's a simple kiss. I get that he's queer. I'm queer too, but for God's sake this is a performance. He acts like he's pressing his lips against a slug. Pretend I'm a hot guy if you have to. I literally do not care. Just be professional."

Jack laughs and turns up the music.

I may not be into show choir but nothing makes me happier than singing, except maybe hanging out with these two, so I sip on the cinnamon latte and sing my face off.

I almost forget about the note.

Almost.

I keep it in my pocket and feel its heat between my thumbs.

two

The teacher parking spots are filled with hay bales.

"Senior prank day." Jack brightens. They love mischief of all kinds. "It's an ag theme. Do you like it?"

The principal is a pretty good sport about senior pranks as a rule, but she herniates over parking lot traffic flow on a good day, and so this has sent her over the edge. She's currently standing on top of her car trying to direct parents to a diverted path while frantically pointing at the incoming staff, yelling at them to move the hay.

"Now *this* is my frequency," Turtle says.

"Chaos?" I say.

"Freedom, young one! Freedom!"

She pulls into her usual spot under the tree in the back parking lot and we all jump out. The whole school is a mess. Banners and posters celebrating the seniors are everywhere. Mr. Ortiz, the driver's ed teacher, is lurching down the hall like a zombie covered in water from some kind of booby trap.

"I did that," Jack says, all swagger. "Set it up myself so it would go *sploosh* all over him."

"Poor guy," I say.

"I don't forgive him for making me parallel park for two hours straight before he would sign my driver's test paper."

"He is a little overeager, it's true."

"And push-ups if you didn't look in your side mirror before turning?" Turtle adds. "Is that even legal?"

"Coach's office is in the bathroom!" Cecelia Torres laughs, skipping by, wet from being tagged with a water balloon. "Like, his desk is in there and everything. He's all pissed."

"That was me, for I am a genius," Turtle says, giving a curtsy. "You're welcome. Victor helped me carry the desk."

Maybe she sees something in my expression I can't quite hide, because she slings an arm over my shoulder so sandalwood and ylang-ylang rises between us. "Sorry you couldn't come help us. It was a total bore-slash-drag if I'm being honest."

"No it wasn't. You had the best time ever."

"You know we would have brought you but—"

"I know, I know," I say, "seniors only."

"It's never as fun without you. Promise triple swear." She squeezes me.

Feathers float through the air and the halls have gone way beyond their usual controlled hum. Music blares from a bunch of classrooms and people are just throwing down because they're young and it always seems like the end of the world. Summer is really coming and I feel like I'm one of those feathers, riding on air, untethered.

When we get to our lockers I jump up and drag a streamer from the ceiling, wrap it around my neck, then sink down and pull out my math homework. My math final is tomorrow. We're reviewing now and I can't remember much from the beginning of the semester. I really haven't understood any of it since the end of algebra I two years ago.

"You okay?" Turtle examines me and I have this unsettling feeling she and Jack are trying to take care of me.

I don't want to be taken care of. I want to take care of myself.

"I'm good. Just have to finish this before class starts."

Jack peers over my paper. "Do you need help?"

"It's moon runes," I say. "Too late for me. Save yourself."

"Don't worry." Turtle takes out her copy of *Economics Today* and trades it for *The Fire Next Time*, then slaps her locker shut. "They said you would be a little hazy. It should wear off tomorrow."

I furrow my brows. "What do you mean 'hazy'? Who's 'they'?"

Jack coughs. Loudly.

Turtle blanches. "You have your orange juice, right?" she asks.

"Yeah. Did you put all that juice in my backpack?"

"What? No!"

"Well why are you micromanaging my orange juice intake?"

"*Uch*," she says. "What kind of question is that? Dehydration is a major problem. Also, it affects your skin. Just drink some, okay? It'll make me feel better about your chances of battling premature aging. Plus vitamin C!"

I go back to trying to figure out the problem in front of me.

"If you need help studying let me know," Jack says. "I'm here for you."

I scribble some nonsensical answers across my worksheet just so there are answers where there are supposed to be. "Thanks," I tell them.

"You're sure you're good?" Turtle says.

"Yes. OMG, guys, please. Get outta here," I say in Gran's accent.

"Goodbye, sweetie pie," Jack says.

They tip their hat and Jack and Turtle lock arms and head down the hall away from me. Jack looks back. So they're talking about me. So what?

I wander to my seat in algebra II, dead center in the classroom. This is strategic. Everyone gets lost in the middle. I like to be lost, especially in this class where people are tripping over themselves to prove they're smart.

A whine starts up in my ear. I slap it just as Opal Crow sits down next to me. She gives me a sharp look and pulls out her phone.

"You ever get the feeling something's going on and you don't know what it is?" I say.

Opal smiles. "Sure. Isn't that just life? I basically never have any idea what's happening. It just is . . . happening."

"I guess so. But now I feel like I've lost something and I don't know what it is."

"Don't go looking for it." Opal pulls her tablet and homework from her bag.

"Can you hear a ringing noise?" I ask.

"Now?"

"Yeah."

Opal shakes her head.

"All right," Mrs. Dale says, holding up one hand. "Can I have everyone's attention in four–three–two–one." The chattering and rustling stop. "There we go. We're going to get started with our end-of-semester reviews. If you don't have your worksheets out yet, please get them so we can go over the problems together."

The whining starts up again and I slap at my ear.

"You better get your shit together, girl," Opal whispers.

We have an open campus and after lunch some of the kids are coming in with Starbucks or Sonic, and some obviously stoned with bags of Cheetos in hand. Some of the Native kids hang out front listening to music from one of those new portable speaker watches, and then file in talking and laughing. For my part, I couldn't get myself to go to the lawn with Turtle and Jack where all their friends were applying highlighter to one another and reading work from some new poet they discovered, so I spent lunch in the back by myself staring at the note.

All sorts of ominous theories about the note have started creeping into my consciousness. Someone is going to kidnap me off the bus. Someone is stalking me and is going to shank me on the bus. Someone is messing with my head and wants to make me late for finals and ruin my life and my chances of passing my junior year by making me get on a bus instead of going to school. Someone is in my room right now and Gran is in danger.

With effort, I shake them all off.

"So about tomorrow," Turtle says when we're all back at our lockers. "We'll meet you at the Mountain for coffee after rehearsal and then go back to my house and do face masks and whatever." She pulls out a couple of notebooks (because she is the last remaining human on earth who insists on being analog), beat up and battered after nine months of use. "You sure you don't want a party? We could have the crew over, do a sundae bar or something—"

"Sundae bar?"

"Well I don't know."

"No," I say.

"Sundae bars are fun and totally retro. My mom even knows where to find gummy bears and some of the other candy they canceled a while back."

"No."

"Okay, but we're making you a cake!"

"I don't need a cake," I say. "Gran's got it covered."

"Oh right. Cake for breakfast," Turtle says.

Cake for breakfast has been a birthday tradition in my house for as long as I can remember. Even before Mom died Gran would be at the house first thing in the morning like it was Christmas or something. Mom and Dad would stumble out of bed and we would all eat cake together. Best breakfast ever.

"So we're on," Jack says. "Turtle can plan the perfect girls' soiree and we'll have an awesome birthday night with you." They look at their phone. "Ugh. Time to pay the piper."

Sure enough, the bell rings.

Olive Duran is a small roundish woman with hair as white and curly as a French poodle's and bright purple fingernails. She used to be my neighbor before Dad left and I moved in with Gran. Mom once took care of her house a long time ago when she and her husband went out of town on a cruise to watch the last of the whales. I don't remember much except their house was covered in books and pictures and that when I opened up the refrigerator, instead of condiments there were rows and rows of red and purple nail polish and a few packs of double-A batteries. When she speaks her voice is sweet and higher pitched than it looks like it should be, but not in a squeaky way, in a soft, fuzzy way.

This class is special. Mrs. D uses a real darkroom instead of everything being digital. There's only space for fifteen students and you get to check out a camera and film. I have loved every second of it. I think. For some reason right now I'm drawing a blank about the semester.

Mrs. D has retrieved a yardstick from the corner of the room and is using it both as a cane and for emphasis. She taps it against the floor now to get everyone's attention. "Hello! Okay, oh how nice of you to pay attention when I speak. Just lovely. Thank you." She smiles. "We're going to be assembling our collage all week in preparation for the bank gallery presentation, which will run all summer. Portfolios are over there." She points to the far wall. "Pick between three and five images you'd like to use in the collage and we'll begin the assembly process. Remember none of this will happen without collaboration so leave your little egos at the door."

Collage. That's right. The class is putting together meaningful photographic moments from the school year and they'll be up in the community bank over the summer.

"How it's assembled is up to you, but you'll use what you've done in class up to now. I've got the glue and the clear paint to seal it and you'll need my approval before doing anything permanent." Mrs. D taps the yardstick twice on the ground and everyone in class goes over to their portfolios and then to one of the big tables in the center of the room to organize themselves. "We only have two more classes so let's get cracking."

I follow my classmates to the corner where the portfolios are lined up and find mine, my name written in silver Sharpie in the bottom left corner. It looks and feels familiar but is also like a figment of my own imagination. I take it back to the table and start thumbing through it. There are only a few pictures in here, and they're of Turtle and Jack hugging by the river, snow at their feet. I remember taking them there back when I was first playing with the camera. We went to Angel Wing Bridge that day too, wind whipping us around, snow sitting thick on the ground. These were only test pics. It's been a whole semester since then. I flip through the empty plastic pages of the portfolio. They're smudged and imperfect, like something was in here at some point.

"Mrs. Duran, where's my stuff?" I ask, lifting the portfolio off the table so she can see it.

Sunlight floods the room in rectangular streams that splash over the empty plastic sheets and for a moment I am lost in it.

"For heaven's sake," Mrs. D says, snapping me back to now. She's sifting through a pile of photographs on one of the desks, refusing to make eye contact with me. Finally she stops and lets the black-and-white photograph she's holding fall to the side. "I won't penalize you for your missing work. I'm sure you'll still have plenty to contribute. You've got a good eye. You can go and help your classmates get themselves organized." She points. "And you've got a couple of good pictures left if I recall."

She smiles and it is not a smile.

"Mrs. Duran?"

"Yes?" She looks at me over her glasses like she wishes I would leave her alone.

I also wish I could leave her alone. But I can't. "What do you mean 'left'? Do you have my pictures? Did they just disappear?"

Jenny Lawrence looks up from across the room, interest painted across her features.

"Mind your business," Mrs. Duran snaps.

Jenny shrugs and looks away.

Mrs. Duran closes the space between us.

"You're saying I did the assignment and these pages look like they've been used, but I don't remember taking pictures or what they were about. It's like the whole semester has disappeared. Except look!" I show her my evidence. The smudged pages, how they look so different from the few at the end that appear entirely untouched. "There were pictures in here, right?"

I know the expression on her face. That's pity, wide open and obvious.

"You did the assignment," she says.

"So where is it?"

She pats me on the arm. "There will be no penalty to your grade. Now go help your classmates."

three

Mrs. Duran lied to me. Or if she didn't lie, she omitted.
I know she did.

Sometimes I wait for Turtle and Jack at the end of the day if it's bad weather so I can get a ride home. I think again about the rusted red truck sitting in my apartment complex parking lot, about why I don't drive it. I know it belonged to my dad and he left it with me when he moved to Florida after Mom died. But I don't know why I don't drive it or why I carry around the keys in my bag, or why I would put myself in a position where I have to get rides all the time when I hate relying on other people for anything.

Even though I don't understand myself or my own reasoning about driving, I do know why I like to watch Jack and Turtle in show choir. Because it's entertaining and amazing in basically every way.

I'm delighted to find that by the time I get to the auditorium, Turtle and Kevin are about to end their duet, which means I'm going to get to see the famous awkward kiss. This is already an improvement over my photography class, which I spent cutting out other people's pictures since I didn't have any of my own.

The music stops and the whole auditorium goes silent. This situation with Kevin and Turtle has become a joke for show choir kids and they're just waiting for the punch line.

Kevin always delivers.

He leans toward Turtle, puckering hard so his mouth looks like a tiny butthole. His eyes widen and Turtle looks out toward the audience.

"Are you going to do something about this?" She squints into the darkness, hand over her eyes to block the light.

"No. You're right. You're right, Turtle. Kevin," Mr. Lovett calls out, waving his hands. "Stop it. Just stop. It's not going to work if you look like you're afraid she's going to eat you. She's not a praying mantis, Kevin. She's not going to decapitate you on contact."

"I know she's not. It's just awkward, okay?" Now that the threat of a kiss is diminished, Kevin looks less like he's going to pass out. Some color is returning to his cheeks.

"No one forced you to audition, Kevin," Mr. Lovett says. "No one held a gun to your head. You knew this was part of the deal."

"You literally made me audition," Kevin says. "You came to my house and begged." Kevin looks the part. He's tall and princely in a totally colonial-era-admiral kind of way.

"I could eliminate the kiss—"

Cries of protest come from all directions.

"I'm not afraid to kiss," Kevin says glumly.

"Oh for shit's sake. You just press your lips together," Mr. Lyle says. "And before that you sing the lines assigned to you without sounding like you're about to dive into a lion's mouth." He clutches his forehead. "The die is cast, my friend. You're in now and you've got to learn to kiss this girl in a way that doesn't make you look imperiled." He turns to the seat next to his. "I wouldn't normally do this, but could you please go demonstrate? Nothing too X-rated, just a nice kiss like you love the girl."

"I do love the girl," Jack says. They stand, crack their knuckles. Titters ensue.

He nudges Jack. "Go on. Go."

Jack gets up and wipes their hands on their pants. They push up their sleeves and do a couple jumping jacks.

"Oh thanks," Turtle drawls.

"Hang on, let me do some push-ups," Jack says.

"Now, now," Mr. Lovett tuts.

Jack climbs the side stairs until they're in front of Turtle. Kevin moves out of the way. Jack is in jeans and a black T-shirt, their leather bracelets on one wrist, hair flopping about messily. My heart lurches when Turtle and Jack look at each other. I want that. I hope someday I can have it.

"Okay," Mr. Lyle says. "Let's get this show on the road, people."

"You go," Jack says. "Sing the last few bars again."

Turtle clears her throat and then her lovely voice echoes through the auditorium. "To be alone with me . . . to be alone with you."

Turtle nuzzles Jack's palm theatrically.

"Good, good," Mr. Lovett says. "Now the kiss. Are you watching this, Kevin?"

Kevin *is* watching, uncomfortably, from the side.

Jack leans forward slowly, pulling Turtle flush against their own body, and they melt into a deep kiss.

"Uh," Mr. Lovett says, clapping twice to make them stop, which they do, but barely. "You don't have to do it quite like that, but you get the idea." He turns his attention back to Kevin. "See how Jack was moving toward her, not trying to escape her as they were kissing?"

"They are *together!*" Kevin yells.

Jack and Turtle pull apart, laughing, still looking deeply at each other.

I have seen Jack and Turtle kiss a million times at least, but something about it fills me with a sadness too big to hold alone. It overwhelms me and before I can cry—no, sob—no, throw myself on the ground and beg someone to take it away, I drag myself out and run for the bathroom, backpack thumping. I get into a stall just in time for the contents of my lunch to make it into the toilet bowl. Nothing about this day feels right.

Something is so wrong with me.

When I get home, Eunice is waiting for me at the front door, with her little black Mohawk and her one arthritic paw. She's bouncing up and down like a jackhammer, keeping her right leg off the floor. You'd think Gran wasn't home most of the day, that she's been alone since I left this morning, but Gran goes to work at 2 p.m. only three days a week. A couple of hours home alone isn't even long enough for Eunice to have to pee. Gran has been doing extra shifts lately though. Maybe Eunice knows. Maybe she's grown lonely.

I'm tired but Eunice is cute, so I take her for a walk. She prances hither and thither, pants joyfully, poops next to an empty flower planter, and when we get back she paces around in front of Gran's craft room spinning in circles. I'm already settled on the couch with the TV on, totally ready to zone out until I can disappear the day, but Eunice is growling, barking, whimpering . . . anything to get my attention. Finally I get up and go to her.

"What's in there, pup?" I say.

Eunice's tail slaps against the floor and her tongue lolls out of the right side of her mouth. She whimpers and scoots around like she's waiting for me to turn the knob. This room is reserved for Gran. She has projects going all the time and she doesn't want anyone in there messing with her stuff. This is Gran's small joy. She should be retiring from nursing and crafting her little heart out. She should have retired a long time ago.

I feel the familiar tug of guilt. She can't retire because she's got me to take care of now, a kid she didn't expect to have.

But here I am! Ta-da! No retirement for you!

Shaddap, Gran says with a kiss on the top of my head when I tell her I'd rather eat Ramen forever than have her work to support me. *It's not your business.*

Eunice barks.

"Okay," I say. "But only to prove to you there's nothing in there. And you stay out here."

The last thing I need is for Gran to come home to Eunice in a ribbon nest. I start to open the door, expecting to find piles of wool, Gran's loom, wrapping paper, scrapbooks, and everything else I remember being in here.

The room looks nothing like it's supposed to.

Fear clamps down on me and I back away. I feel like I'm in the wrong apartment. This is not where I'm supposed to be. Everything is suddenly unfamiliar. I make myself look again. There's no worktable and bench. There's no canvas and no paint. It's a bedroom. A regular one with a sleigh bed and a white duvet with small purple flowers on top. Posters plaster the walls. Eunice looks up at me, tail whipping against the floor as she pants, offering up her one lame paw.

The world brightens around me, overexposed and harsh. My stomach twists and my mouth fills with water. It's so sudden and so bad that I have to steady myself, press my forehead against the white wood, grip the metal to hold myself upright or I would fall to the floor like I did this morning.

A person does not forget what an entire room looks like in their own house.

Tomorrow I will tell Gran I need to see a doctor. I will tell her the world has stopped making sense and something is wrong with my brain.

I'll tell her if I make it through the night.

Eunice whines.

I peek in the room one more time, see the pink carpet, the white desk, the silver frame on it, but when I try to focus on the picture in the frame, I think I'm going to die. I see spots. My stomach twists again as though it's wringing itself out and

I close the door quickly and sit on the floor, my back against the plush gray sofa that's covered in Gran's black lace shawl. Just touching something that touches Gran on a regular basis makes me feel better, like I am where I'm supposed to be and the entire universe isn't out to get me.

But still.

A smell has followed me, flowery and milky all at once.

A sob escapes against my will and without any warning.

Eunice sits in front of me and watches me carefully. She's been with me a long time. Before Mom died. Before Dad left. We got her when I was five, walked into the Dogs Without Borders animal shelter here in Old Town. She was just a puppy then, and was already hopping on three legs, unable to use the fourth due to some mysterious condition. She wasn't even cute. Eunice is the kind of adorable that takes you by surprise over time. They put us in the room with the puppies and let them all run around. I knew Eunice was the one right away. She made room for the others. She waited for me to call her over. She was patient.

She's not looking so patient now.

My breathing slows from the memory. There's so much I seem to have forgotten; having this one piece of myself, whole, helps the rest of me to calm down. I let my eyes close as Eunice nudges my hand over her head. I pet her and the nausea dissipates with every breath.

When I've recovered enough to be sure I'm not going to pass out or vomit on the floor, I look at the closed door again, cheap painted white wood. The next door over is the bathroom, then there's my room, then there's Gran's, every wall of the apartment covered in paintings of nude ladies and bolts of silk and satin. The floors are hardwood with jute area rugs and corners decorated in pottery from all over the globe.

The grains in the wood separate in front of me and come back together.

I don't need to see the inside of that room. I should get as far away from it as possible.

Eunice looks up at me and gives another bark.

"No, I don't," I tell her. "Leave it alone."

The door quavers in my peripheral vision like it's alive.

I turn my back on it now, go into the small kitchen and get myself one of the cold sparkling waters Gran keeps in there. I catch sight of a chocolate cake on the second shelf, the top covered in raspberries, and I remind myself I'm probably under a lot of stress because of school ending and Turtle and Jack leaving and everything. Plus, tomorrow is my birthday. I'll be seventeen years old. I rub the can on my forehead and then across my own cheeks.

There's sweat on my upper lip.

I go into my room to lie down but as soon as I'm down I want to be up. My body won't settle. Eunice pads in and leaps on my bed, turns several circles and then rests her chin on her paws.

"Eunice," I say, "this is the worst."

I thought a night alone would be a relief, but it's not. I hate it. I want to be watching a movie with Jack and Turtle, even if they insist on making out every five minutes; I want to sit at the table and talk to Gran about my day. Anything but be alone.

I pull off my clothes and get ready to shower because a shower seems like it would feel really good and warm my bones, and as my pants fall to the floor, the paper flutters out of my pocket and lands at my feet.

MEET ME ON THE LITTLE BLUE BUS
7:45 a.m. 5/19/32

Tomorrow is the day.

The day I may or may not get on the little blue bus.

I go to my closet to get some sweats and a T-shirt. It's packed with neatly folded houndstooth, corduroy, linen, and an entire shelf of button-down shirts on one side. I look under the jewelry box where I found the piece of paper, hoping there will be something else, some hint of what it means. There's nothing, but I see something behind the scarves dangling from their hanger. I push the scarves to the side, and I lose all my breath. It's a picture, stuck to the wall behind my clothes.

"Oh shit," I say as I thump onto the floor, struck by another breathtaking stomach somersault. I exhale through it, one hand clawing into the beige carpet underneath me until the feeling steadies and I can see clearly again. The solid earth seems to upend itself, to reach for me.

I steel myself and focus.

"Stop," I tell myself. "Stop it."

Eunice thumps her tail against the bed but doesn't move.

You will look at this picture, Blue, she seems to be saying. *You will look at it with your right eyes.*

I take a deep, slow inhale and look at the picture. It's me

with four children, three boys and a girl. They're younger and browner than me, none of them more than twelve. I blink hard and look again. They are right there with me, clutched into my side as close in as family, and yet I don't recognize any of them.

Now that the picture has come into focus I can't stop looking at it. I peel it carefully from the wall. It might have been taken in the summer, judging from all the green grass and the blooming garden in the background. I think I see something, maybe a pool, off in the distance behind me. Mountains farther behind that. I know that mountain range. That's here in Owl Nook, and unless I have a twin I don't know about, that's me.

And yet I have no memory of any of it whatsoever.

I don't recognize anyone in it, maybe least of all myself. One of the boys is making a face, sticking out his tongue. Another is giving the camera the finger so subtly you would have to look as closely as I am to be able to see it. Two of the boys are so interchangeable they must be twins. The girl has her arms around my waist and is smiling huge, her hair pulled back so tightly into braids that her eyes stretch.

I touch my hair. It's about a quarter-inch thick like I shaved it recently. It feels soft and fuzzy. In the picture, my eyes are shining coal. I'm not as thin as I am now and my light cotton harem pants hang loosely off my hips, tan belly exposed, a cropped black linen button-down on top. My hair is almost down to my butt and it's black and thick and beautiful. I know I had long hair. That seems right. And I know now I have almost no hair. But how do you not remember cutting it all off?

My phone buzzes. I look down at the screen.

GRAN
You okay, sweetheart?

Gran always knows when something is off.

                                              ME
                                    Yes, ma'am. You?

GRAN
Lydia's being an asshole. Tell you about it later.

                                              ME
                                      Can't wait.

GRAN
Don't stay up too late. We have a date early in the morning,
kid.

                                              ME
                            How could I forget? Love you.

GRAN
Love you.

I almost feel normal when I'm done texting that last message to Gran. I slap on one of the sleep patches Gran leaves me
for when I've got anxiety and can't fall asleep. It's all natural
and Gran says it's better than staring at the ceiling all night.

Even with the sleep patch it still takes me forever before my eyes start to droop like my body is as awake as it is tired. I let the sounds of my neighborhood sing me to sleep. Mrs. Jenkins is upstairs dancing to her old-school music. She's roughly nine hundred years old but she's a night owl, and her footsteps remind me there's always someone there besides Eunice if I need help. Mrs. Jenkins is tough. An ambulance passes outside. Enrique from 1A laughs. It's big and booming. Downstairs, Lori and Joseph start arguing and then go quiet. My toes begin to tingle.

I think of the look Mrs. Duran gave me in photography class, my missing pictures, the puking in the bathroom at school when I saw Turtle and Jack kissing like that, Gran's craft room, even a haircut I can't remember—all of it adds up to something I can't understand. As I warm and drowse, I think again of the piece of paper. Someone deliberately stuck a picture to my wall *inside* my closet. Someone's been in my room.

Gran says all it takes is a good night's sleep to turn an upside-down world right side up again. If you're pissed off about something or fighting with someone, it all looks clear in the light of day.

It's a nice idea, but I'm pretty sure it won't work. Not this time.

four

I'm pushed out of sleep in a panic, my fingernails clawing at my own sheets as desperately as if I've been dropped into a hole and am falling at a billion miles per minute, scratching for solid ground. I don't know how I got here or where here is or when I fell asleep last night. It's only after I've been awake for several seconds that I realize my alarm is sounding from the bedside table beside me and I'm not falling and the impact of the kind I imagined is not imminent.

Also, my phone is belting out the classic song "As Long as You Love Me" by Justin Bieber, which Jack programmed into it like a month ago because they like to rub my nose in my monster eighth-grade crush and the fact that he's so old now. They stole my phone and the next morning when my alarm went off I lost my shit and then I left it because the truth is I love that song. Jack for sure doesn't have any boundaries so maybe they left the note and Photomagicked the picture or something. Turtle and Jack have been pranking a lot lately. Maybe there's a rational explanation. Anyway, it's pretty hard to be super freaked out when the Biebs is playing. Plus it's daytime and I can see the tree outside my window and it's a pretty green.

I look at my screen. It's all full of emojis and messages from Jack and Turtle. Sometimes I think I should diversify my friend group beyond the two of them, but then, why bother? I've already peaked.

TURTLE
OH MY GOSH YOU'RE SEVENTEEN!

JACK
HAPPY BIRTHDAY BABY!

TURTLE
WE LOVE YOU

TURTLE
WE'RE GOING TO BRING YOU SO MUCH COFFEE

JACK
WE'RE GOING TO CARRY YOU INTO SCHOOL ON A DAIS LIKE THE GODDESS YOU ARE

I can hear Gran in the kitchen. I'm not dizzy anymore and I don't feel like I'm going to puke either. I get to my feet and test them. They hold me up. All good.

It's a relief to see my grandmother. I've never stopped fangirling over her because she's literally the coolest. Gran's got hair dyed as black as mine, which she says is only fair since I got it from her in the first place. She wears animal print on occasion and lipstick no matter what. She wears lipstick *to bed*. She's from Sheepshead Bay in Brooklyn so she's got this thick accent she's totally in denial about and her favorite beverage is Campari and soda. She spends most of her life saving people while also being their personal counselor. She took me in when Mom died in a freak skiing accident, because my dad moved to Florida after Mom's accident and I didn't want to move there, and he left me instead of sticking around for the hard part, so fuck him. Mom dying was sad and terrible and is always in the air between us, and we try not to talk about it.

Lately, we try not to talk about much of anything.

Right now Gran's in a black lace robe and a satin slip and is listening to the news, yammering along with it, saying things like "that's right" and "you tell 'em." Gran looks me up and down. "Happy birthday, sweetheart."

"Doesn't Eunice need to go out?"

"No. I took her."

"In a slip?"

"What do you want from me? I put on a coat. That's as good as it's going to get." She makes a shooing motion at me. "Go on. No one knows about a slip under a coat, do they, pumpkin?"

Eunice comes over to her, shaking her tail so hard her entire backside wiggles. Gran pets her. She is such a good gran she gets up to see me off to school every day, even when she gets home from work at two in the morning. She pulls out a chair for me and I sit down. Gran yawns loudly. "Another week and I'll be on the day shift. I put in the request but they can't do it yet. Feliz and her maternity leave are doing me in. Why do they have to pick on an old lady?" She pads to the fridge and pulls out the chocolate cake. "My favorite breakfast." She smiles. "What do you say? You ready, you big seventeen-year-old?"

"I missed you last night."

She turns the sound down on the radio, furrows her brow. "You missed me? I missed you too. Sure would have liked to be home with you instead of with Lydia the asshole." She frowns. "Are you okay?"

"I'm good now."

"You know you can always call Mrs. J, right? She'll always come hang out with you if you need someone."

"I know. It wasn't like that. I . . . I don't need a babysitter. It was more like in my mind."

"Are you depressed?"

"I don't think so."

She touches my forehead. "Your head's not hot. Hold on, I'll get you a compress."

"I'm not depressed and I'm not sick. I promise. There's literal chocolate cake that I'm about to eat."

"Depression is more complicated than cake," she says confidently. "I got candles. But first, a real hug. Not the good-morning kind. The birthday kind that means something."

I sink into her bosom. I'm so short and she's so tall, I'll never not feel like a little kid when this happens, which is as often as possible. When she's hugged me long enough to be satisfied, she slaps a couple of plates onto the table and retrieves some forks.

"You do the honors while I get my coffee. I'd offer you some but I know you like that fancy shit." She pours me a glass of orange juice, setting it in front of me.

"That reminds me, I've been meaning to talk to you about that. Did you put orange juice in my backpack yesterday?"

Gran looks up, but barely. "Yeah. I don't want you to dehydrate."

"People keep saying that."

"You need to drink a big glass. You're supposed to have half your weight in ounces plus another eight ounces." She hands me a giant knife and I cut us both a slice. "Go on. Drink."

"Now?"

"Well yeah!"

"But orange juice and chocolate cake?"

"Drink," she insists.

"Okay, fine." I take a few sips. "So what happened with Lydia?" I ask when she finally sits down across from me, looking a little more relaxed. Lydia is Gran's best friend and also her sometime work nemesis.

"Heh?"

"You told me she was being an asshole last night?"

"She's always some sort of asshole. It's her thing." Gran shrugs. "Sometimes when I'm working it seems like everyone is an asshole, but by the time I leave there I forgive them because I realize I'm an asshole too. And now it doesn't even matter. It's like dust off my shoulder because now you're my big seventeen-year-old girl. I can't believe it."

A couple of tears hover in the corners of her eyes.

"You okay, Gran?"

"I'm okay. It's just all a lot and the older I get the more I realize it's never going to not be a lot."

"Life, you mean?"

"Yeah. Life is what I mean. Watching you get older. Watching me get older too. It's all a lot. *Uch.*" She sniffs and sticks a single candle into my piece of cake. "Make a wish and fuck all the rest. And make it a good one. You deserve a really good wish to come true."

I wish to know who left me the note and who put that picture in my closet. Other than that, I could only wish for Jack and Turtle never to leave me and for Gran to live forever, and maybe for Mom to come back and those things aren't going to happen.

Oh, and true love.

I wish for that.

The cake is amazing and we both groan when we take our first bites.

"You're like a genius," I tell her.

"Me? Oh please. I paid Mrs. Jenkins fifty bucks to bake while I snuck in a nap. She only wanted forty but I threw in an extra ten for her to put mousse in the layers." Gran watches me for a minute, then takes a sip of coffee. "I got a ping last night." Gran is always getting pings. That's what she calls it when she receives a psychic message. She thinks she has the shine because she's Italian and she's pretty sure I have it too. She got a ping when my mom died, a ping when I got a bad grade on a test and didn't tell her about it, a ping when I first brought Turtle home from school with me. It was a day Gran and Mom were sitting at the kitchen table like they used to, gossiping and leaning their heads together. Gran beckoned me over while Turtle was taking off her shoes.

That's a forever, friend, Gran said. *I have a ping!*

"You be careful today," she says now. "Something's not quite right. I can feel it."

This is the language of people who have lost. They always feel the need to tell each other to be vigilant, to take care of themselves, because the last thing a person wants is yet another hurt to add to the mix.

"Okay, Gran." I kiss her cheek. "You going to bed?"

"I might try to stay awake for *The Daily Scoop.*"

"Okay. I'm going to get ready."

"Fine, leave me all alone all by myself."

"Gran!"

"I'm kidding." She hugs me again then stands back and does the thing where she squeezes my cheeks between her palms and stares deeply. "You're looking so much like your mother," she says longingly. "You know that?"

My mother. Long straight black hair, round cheeks, laughing black eyes. "Thanks, Gran," I say.

Then Gran can't look at me anymore and I can't look at her either. She throws a hand on her lower back to demonstrate to me how much it aches, and starts fumbling in a cabinet.

"Love you," I say.

She doesn't turn around. "You call me if you need something today," Gran says. "Anything, understand?"

I understand. And I do need something. I can feel it in every cell.

I just don't know what it is.

five

I'm outside my apartment where I usually wait for Turtle and Jack, but instead of staying there like I'm supposed to, instead of waiting for the rumble of her Jeep, I'm walking. Where my street intersects with the main town artery, I can see a train of cars heading for school or work.

People.

Movement.

It's like I know what I'm doing but I don't want to admit to myself that I'm doing it because if I do I may stop and I don't want to stop. I don't look back. I feel driven and it's satisfying to do what my gut is telling me to do instead of the things my head is telling me to do. I turn the corner onto the main road, then cross into the post office parking lot, to the bus stop, and only when I'm tucked into the bus shelter does my heart rate begin to slow.

I'm the only one there. I sit and hold the metal rails on the side of the shelter that are there to help people who can't stand up easily, but in this case the bar is helping to keep me from fleeing. Right on time, a little blue bus scoots down the lane, stopping and starting, puttering along, taking its time.

I want it to hurry.

I can imagine Turtle pulling up to the curb with my birthday coffee, being confused, and Jack running up the stairs to find me. I can imagine Gran and Eunice getting scared because they don't know where I went and for Gran that's the worst thing in the world.

I tap out a quick text. DON'T NEED A RIDE THIS MORNING! SEE YOU AT THE MOUNTAIN! Then I go back to watching the bus.

Theories from yesterday give way to newer, less horrible ones like maybe the piece of paper I found in my closet was a joke and maybe there's a surprise party waiting for me on this bus and the entire show choir is going to do a huge number and Kevin will finally kiss the girl.

I have to trust that the part of me that wants to get on the bus and see what comes of it is not a fool and that she knows best.

It's not easy to trust.

The bus pulls in front of me and the doors swing open.

"Blue," the bus driver says when I hesitate, bobble between my feet. "What happened to your hair?"

I lean in toward the bus, one foot on a step. "Did you just call me by my name?"

"Whose name were you hoping for?" The bus driver, whose eyes droop pleasantly at the corners and whose cheeks are whipped with wrinkles, smiles at me. "Got to get going." He signals in the distance. A tall snow-capped mountain sits like a sentry above us. It may be moving toward summer down here, but up there it's stubbornly snowy in patches, so beautiful and dangerous it's an ache. "You coming up?"

I climb the rubber-covered stairs and then pause. "Yes," I say. "Coming up."

"You okay, kiddo?" he asks, when I don't find a seat. I can't make my feet move just yet. There are so many questions I'd like to ask him. "Haven't seen you in a few weeks."

"Weeks?"

"Maybe three? I don't know." He chuckles. "I lose track going up and down all day."

"I think I lost something," I say.

I look up and down the aisle.

No sign of a surprise birthday party or of a reason to get on the bus at all. Maybe it was all some sort of a hoax. Sometimes a piece of paper is just a piece of paper, even when it's mysteriously in your closet.

Except this man who knows me and is looking at me inquisitively when I don't remember him at all and know I've never seen him before in my life—this man and this mystery are reason enough to get on the bus and let it take me away from the day I was supposed to have.

The man nods, glancing at the worn orange band of his watch. "Something you want me to look out for?" He glances at me uncertainly. "Jacket? Gloves? I have a box in the back. We can check it when we get to the top."

"I don't think so." I think I'm freaking this poor guy out, but I'm also freaked out and am not totally sure how to proceed. He knows me and it seems like he knows me more than just a little. "I don't know what it is. That I lost."

"I hope you find it." He taps his watch.

He doesn't ask me any further questions. It's that he has a schedule to keep but also people try to stay out of each other's business around here. Plenty of Owl Nook citizens live where they do because the rest of the world is too nosy or busy or fretful. It strikes a nice balance between city and country, with the big estates on the outskirts of town and the dairy farms and pecan orchards, plus the city center and Old Town where any number of Wild West legends had shootouts at one time or another. Ever since Owl Nook turned out to be a cheap and desirable place for big tech campuses, the town is booming. Not Old Town. Old Town is exactly how it's always been. Live and let live and all that.

There are only two other people on the bus, guys wearing beanies and gloves. They both look like they're going home to bed and not going to work. They're slumped over, almost asleep, and no bother. I don't recognize them or get any feelings about them. I don't think either of them wrote the note in my pocket. Otherwise the bus is clean and empty.

I settle into a seat, weathered but pleasant, and watch as the bus driver plods through Old Town, the part of Owl Nook that remains untouched by progress and instead is evidence of a history all of us would like to forget now. Violence between Native Americans and Conquistadors, the invasion of the white people in the 1960s, the way some people are here for the freedom and the cheap land and the job opportunities and others are here because the red dirt has taken hold under the skin.

I feel this place in my bones, in my breath and my cells. I feel pride that I was born in the hospital where Gran works with the Virgin of Guadalupe statue out front. I love that when I'm driving around with Turtle and Jack we're bad bitches patrolling the streets I know so well and that we play our music loud and know all the checkout people at the grocery store by my house and that Saturdays in the summer people play music off their front porches and sometimes they have block parties and dance in the street.

People come for the close proximity to skiing and the food, but there are also dollar stores and liquor stores and advertisements for local casinos that feel somehow apocalyptic. The roads are full of potholes from where they are filled in and then explode even deeper when the weather changes.

Now the bus crosses over to the west side where the corporations are cropping up against the mountains with fancy new restaurants and coffee shops, car dealerships and gyms with full-service spas and views of the mountain and juice bars downstairs. You almost wouldn't know it was the same place, but all this glass and metal is creeping toward my side of town, little by little.

TURTLE IS CALLING . . .
TURTLE IS CALLING . . .

Shit.

Turtle starts yelling into the phone before I've even had the chance to say hello.

"You're on speaker!" she shouts. We've vowed always to

tell each other right away ever since I let out a string of fucks once when her mom was within earshot. "Why aren't you answering my texts?" Her hair is like an extension of whatever mood she's in and I can see it now, curling and blowing in the wind, charged electric with worry. "Where the fuck are you?"

"I'm fine."

"It's great you're fine," Turtle says. "We're happy you aren't kidnapped or something, but you still didn't answer my question."

"I'm on the little blue bus. You've heard of it? The little blue bus?"

"Of course I've heard of it!"

"There was a note."

"Note? From who?"

"I don't know. It's a mystery. Maybe someone wanted me to take a little ride on my birthday."

"You can't just take off like that. After what happened last week—"

"What happened?"

"Turtle," Jack says with a warning.

I'm suddenly irritated. "First of all, I'm my own person and can do what I want. Second of all, something really off is happening, like mega super off. You think I haven't noticed all your *looks*, your things you're throwing out there that don't make sense? And what is with the orange juice? Do you know I've passed out twice and puked and had this ringing in my ear since yesterday morning?"

The two guys are looking at me with interest now so I lower my voice.

"So what is going on?"

"Oh God, oh shit, she's gone rogue," Turtle says. "What do we *do*?"

"Rogue? How can I go rogue when I have no idea what's even happening? So I found this note and maybe it's nothing but maybe it's somehow related and either way since no one will be honest with me and it's my birthday I'm not getting off this bus. Understood?"

"Blue, you're right," Jack says.

"Jack!" Turtle yells.

"What? There's no point in lying to her. They said there was a chance it wouldn't take right and it didn't take." I picture Jack stroking Turtle's wrist to get her to calm down. "We'll just go get her. It's cool. Nothing has even happened yet. Blue, tell us where you are and we'll meet you at the next stop. We'll explain everything."

"I can't handle this right now, okay?" Turtle says. "I need things to calm down, to go as planned. I'm going to miss my *final* and then my mom is literally going to set me on fire. You promised, Blue. You promised me there wouldn't be any more of this. No more drama, remember?"

I want to feel bad about whatever I did that's upsetting Turtle right now, but I don't know what it is so I can't. When I try to think of some terrible and dramatic thing I've done I draw a total blank.

"I don't remember," I say truthfully. "There's a lot I don't remember. That's what it feels like. That's a part of what's happening, right?"

The hissing whine from yesterday starts up again in my head. My skull feels like it's trying to break apart.

"It's not safe," Turtle says. "None of this is safe."

"Your location, Blue," Jack says. "If you please."

The bus is turning toward the mountain and my insides feel like hot, bitter tea. Maybe they're right and it's time to give up on this. Nothing is happening, the note was some kind of joke, and I should just go to school and have a regular birthday. "I don't want to tell you. I want to go to the mountain."

"But why?" Turtle whines.

"Because I do."

"I'm going to put myself in a high-speed blender, I swear to goddess," Turtle says.

"Turtle, our English final is in thirty minutes," Jack says.

Turtle growls in frustration, then lets out a loud "Fuck!"

"This is what she wants." Jack pauses like they do when they're searching for words. "You can't control everything. You said you don't want any more drama. How dramatic is it going to be if we miss our final? Like you said, your mom's not exactly in a good headspace about this kind of thing now. Let her go."

"Fuckity fuck," Turtle says.

Ever since I can remember, school has been Turtle's everything. She used to get picked on for it, but now that she's in high school and has found a pack of people who accept her for all her academic and club obsessions, she's thriving. Turtle got a scholarship that guarantees her a spot in med school. She's going to be getting thoroughly educated for the max amount of time, with residencies. Missing a final isn't on the docket. Apparently it is for me and I can't say I'm sorry. I can't say I give any shits at all.

"Okay, we're turning around," Turtle says.

"Okay," I say with some relief. Then, "Turtle, you sound exhausted."

"I might be," she says. "I might have gotten there. I should have fetched you a side of antipsychotics to go with your latte, which by the way I am holding in my lap and my crotch is for sure going to get burned any second." Her cup holders are always full of other things. I'm comforted by knowing that. Turtle keeps rubber bands and change in there, and also gum wrappers. Never cups. Turtle blows into her bangs. It's a sound I recognize because she does it so often. "We're still doing your sleepover, right?"

"Yes. I will meet you guys at the Mountain at five no matter what. And I'll call you if anything goes wrong before that."

"Okay." She sounds mollified. "And for the record," she adds, "I knew this wasn't going to work."

"What are you talking about?"

"You'll see."

"Turtle—"

"I'm not trying to be coy, but you will."

The bus pulls over to the side of the road at the top of a hill. We're in a neighborhood I never come to. The houses here have swimming pools and extensive landscaping and people in hats already working with piles of dirt in the yards. There are crocuses all over. The bus door swishes open.

"This just proves my theory," Turtle says.

"What theory?" I say.

"You can't fight city hall."

"Bye, girl," Jack calls. "Have the best birthday ever."

And then with three decisive beeps, they're gone, just as the bus lurches to a stop.

A guy about my age climbs on. He's tall, in work boots, with dark brown hair and warm brown eyes. He's an approachable kind of good-looking, like comfort food or something. I immediately like the way he interacts with his surroundings, the way he takes his time surveying the bus and me, like he was sprouted straight from the earth, like he's the earth itself, nowhere to be, nothing to stress over. But still, when he sees me, his face opens and even though he looks away, back to the driver, his shoulders loosen and a small smile dances across his lips.

"What's up, Rico?" he says to the bus driver, dragging his words with vocal fry.

The boy and Rico bump fists. I'm happy to know Rico's name. Something has been returned to me.

"Going up, my man?" Rico asks.

"Yeah," the boy says. "All the way to the top."

This is a joke they both understand and they share a laugh.

Now the boy begins taking steps toward the back of the bus and I know that's what they are.

Steps toward me.

His eyes are trained on me and they're filled with so much emotion I feel it slapping at me like it's a physical thing. His feelings are big and reaching into me and I want to catch them, hold them, understand them.

Watching him approach, looking at me and away from me at the same time, I feel like I'm falling or spinning or something.

And that's when I know what the note was about and I know what Turtle was talking about and I know what everyone has been hiding from me.

Him.

six

The boy in the blue jacket raises his hand in a greeting and takes the seat across from me. I look him over, more closely this time. It's probably obvious I'm staring at him but I don't care at all. He's tall and on the skinnier side with one of those bodies that looks like it has rubbery ligaments and barely a skeleton keeping him from being absorbed into the floor. His hair is dark brown, not solid black like mine, skin darker than mine. Definitely not white. Or not *just* white. I hate thinking about things like that, but I do because sometimes I think it affects whether or not someone will smile at me or want to talk to me. Most of the time it doesn't but I still think about it. None of that stops me now. I don't look at my lap or my hands. I look at him and how his eyes are soft and kind but his jaw is set, which tells two stories.

"Hey," he says. He seems to have gotten a grip on whatever he was wrestling with as he made his way to his seat, but still, his eyes say he recognizes me. Fear and affection, that's what I see.

Mostly fear.

"Hey," I say back, wanting to also say I'm so glad he sat so close to me so I can look at him more. So I can have this feeling more. So I can feel like a crazy person who is onto something instead of just like a crazy person for whom nothing makes sense. I like this better. Nonsense with hope. "It's my birthday."

"Happy birthday." He assesses my face, my stubbled, nearly bald skull. Then he shakes his head in a movement so small I could have missed it if I wasn't so focused on him. I don't miss it.

And so now without having said much, we have acknowledged something.

He gives a half smile.

It sends so much heat through me knowing that he is looking at me it's like my skin is having an allergic reaction to my own blood flow. I prickle with it.

"My grandmother says the serial killer Ted Bundy was extremely good-looking." Here it comes. Inside Blue who can't shut up when she's nervous. The same Blue that Opal Crow counseled less than twenty-four hours ago to get her shit together. I can try to put on the brakes but she just overrides me, goes flying through red lights and hauls ass into oncoming traffic. "She says a girl should never talk to strangers, that she should have her guard up at all times, that supposedly safe cities where nothing ever happens aside from the occasional accident are the most dangerous of all."

"Are you saying that because you're afraid of me?"

"Wary. I'm wary of good-looking guys."

"I didn't ask you to talk to me," he says.

"I'm just telling you the way girls are indoctrinated. We are taught to be afraid of strangers. But what happens when you meet a stranger who happens to be male and you like him right away? What if he looks like a sheep but he's really a wolf? What if he has a kill kit in the back of his VW bug?"

He shakes his head. "I don't have a VW bug."

I can't tell if he's annoyed by me. I would be. But Inside Blue is at the wheel now and she doesn't care about whether people are annoyed or not, even when she looks at them and wants to slide off her own seat and onto theirs and find out exactly what it would be like to kiss them really hard.

Kissing.

I remember kissing Joe Diaz in sixth grade.

I remember kissing Jacobo Mancini in eighth grade over the summer while on vacation in Italy. I let him put his hands in my bikini bottoms.

I remember playing a game where I was supposed to be in the closet with Calvin Locus and we were supposed to spend six minutes in there and we didn't come out for a much longer time.

I don't remember kissing this boy whose name I don't even know, but my body does. My body positively writhes with knowing. I touch my lips.

My mouth tries to fill with water again, my stomach tries to clench, but I am stronger.

"What are you even saying?" The boy has laughter in his voice, apparently not noticing that I have simultaneously flushed and glazed over. "I remind you of Ted Bundy?"

I try to focus. "He pulled a woman out of a hotel hallway. She had a stomach bug and was going to lie down and was never seen again. He used his looks is what I'm saying."

"Do you think it's a compliment to compare someone to Ted Bundy?"

"Oh no, he was a complete waste of space . . . utter garbage. No. No, that's not what I meant at all."

"Cool," he says, which is dumb but apparently I don't care who is what because I just keep yammering right along.

"You're very good-looking. That's why I'm telling you that about Ted Bundy. I would probably get close enough to an empty trunk that you could knock me out and put me in it."

He snorts.

Now he turns fully toward me with his whole body. The world completely drops away and then something hollow and metallic rises in the back of my throat and the space beneath my belly button is a riot of heat and discomfort.

This is the beginning of a new life.

Everything that came before this is nothing. Starting now is what matters, a whole new chance, a real new beginning.

Mom is dead.

Dad is gone.

Gran is old.

Eunice can barely walk.

This is new.

That's what I think.

The thought finally and mercifully makes Inside Blue shut up.

"No," he says.

"What?" I can't even keep track of my own words so I'm not sure I know everything I've said to him. I've often thought people were good-looking, but I can't say I've ever really been *attracted* to someone before.

He laughs. Probably at me. His teeth are straight and white, the kind of white not a lot of people are born with. I think about where he got on the bus, in the part of town where people have pools, at the top of one mountain, at the foot of another. They have the best views from up there. They have the best teeth up there. I used to live somewhere in the middle. I don't know why where you live matters. I only know it does.

That's my smile, I think, looking at him. *Those are my hands.*

"So if not a serial killer, and by the way a hearty congratulations on that personal accomplishment," I say, "then what are you?"

"Musician," he says. "That's it. Promise. I can't even kill a black widow."

"I believe you," I say firmly. I do believe him.

"Thanks."

"No school?" I say.

"I graduated a year ago," he says.

"And you didn't leave Owl Nook? How intrepid of you."

He gives me a look.

"I mean, obviously you didn't leave," I correct.

He searches my face. "You don't remember *anything?*"

I ignore that because it's easier than digging deeper, and the question makes me queasy.

"How old are you?" I ask.

"You ask a lot of questions."

"You don't want me to ask you questions? Why? Are you thirty or something?"

"Nineteen." He almost laughs.

"Why are you still in Owl Nook?" For a second I wonder if he's one of those guys who's so attached to the mountain he'll spend his life here, drinking, snorting coke, skiing, and rafting. My dad is one of those guys. Or he was before he met my mom. A legendary partier.

"Why does everyone always ask that?" There's an edge to his voice. "Home is home."

"Okay, sorry," I say. "Most people leave."

"Most people are stupid. I don't like that Owl Nook is somewhere people leave as soon as they can. Why?"

"Nothing to do here except sex, drugs, and rock 'n' roll." My mom used to say that.

"That's bullshit. You should be proud to be from here. No place is better than this, and if you don't like it it's your job to make it better. Not to leave like it's something to escape." Then softer, "My dad liked it here. My family is here." He taps a finger on his own thigh. "My dad used to tour when I was little. He was a musician, which is how I became one. This is where he came to rest in between."

"Oh." I'm not so dazzled by him I don't notice he's talking about his dad in the past tense. The past tense is so present all the time. My mother is in the past tense too. That's what I want to tell him.

"I figured it out though. He taught me. My mom too." He pulls a small book from his jacket pocket. *The Flowers of Evil.* "Books help."

"Even ones about evil flowers?"

"Guitar."

"What?"

"That's what I play. For music. My dad did too. He was kind of a big deal in certain circles. Arturo Mendoza. You heard of him?" He waits. I've never heard of him so I have to disappoint him. I don't want to disappoint him.

"No. Sorry. No."

"Never mind. Why would you?"

"That's your job?"

"What?"

"Guitar?"

"Yeah. So far just at restaurants and stuff. But it's okay. I'll get there. I'm going to do it on my own, not just because my dad did."

I don't have any plans or anything at all. I don't have a job because Gran won't let me. She says she wasted all of her high school years working and she wants me to live my life until I have to become an adult. But the thing is that I don't really have a life to live. I drink coffee. I hang out with my friends. I sleep and watch TV. What life? I don't ever want to leave Gran, so life after high school is just a black hole of nothingness.

"Welp, that took about forty-five seconds."

"What?" he says.

"To completely depress myself. My inner voice is an asshole."

"So is mine."

We let that sit between us.

"You ski?" I ask, looking up at the mountain, already knowing the answer. It's all over him, in the brand of jacket he's wearing, his boots, even his hat.

"I board, actually."

I picture him doing this, realizing part of what makes him attractive is the raccoon tan on his cheeks from hours on the mountain. My parents used to have those.

"My mom died in an avalanche skiing out of bounds," I say. "Total freak accident. That's basically life, right? A freak accident. Things just happen. And if things just happen then anything can happen all the time."

He knits his brows. "Out of bounds, huh?"

"Yeah. My parents always did stuff like that. Not anymore though. Anyway, you don't want to hear about all that."

"Sure I do," he says.

I get the free-falling feeling again, like I'm whirling into a vortex at hyperspeed. I don't know what that would feel like, but I imagine it would be something like this, like my stomach trying to escape my mouth. The randomness of everything is too much.

He's not random.

"Can I ask you something?" he says. He's watching me very closely.

"Ask away."

"Why are you going to the mountain at eight a.m. on a Wednesday?"

Pain flickers like fanning pages of a book, but from a distance. It's the distance that disturbs me and produces questions. Why am I on this bus? Why am I talking to this boy? Why does he make me feel old as a bristlecone pine?

"I'm sorry." I don't know what I'm sorry for, but I'm sure that I am.

"Why would you be sorry?"

"I just am."

"So."

"So?"

"Why?"

"Why am I on the bus? Oh." I almost don't tell him, but then I do. "I got a note."

"A note, huh?"

"Yeah, it was in my closet. I thought maybe it was a surprise party or something."

"And what did it say?"

My brain has holes in it like people who do meth, probably. That's what it feels like. Holes important things slip through. "It's very stupid."

"The note is stupid?"

"No, the note's fine. The fact that I got on the bus because of the note is stupid. It's my birthday and the fact that I thought there might be a party—"

"Seems like a reasonable assumption to me. Happy birthday, by the way. So you found a note and it said . . ."

"It said to get on the bus. Today. At this time."

He smiles again. I want him to keep doing that. Every time

he does it, my body gets a little jolt of electricity that feels very good.

"So the note told you to get on the bus in the morning on your birthday and you were all, I'm going to obey the note?"

It's my turn to smile. It doesn't feel as shiny as his but I still realize I haven't done it in a while. "It would appear." I consider. "I would be at school failing algebra II right now. You get a pass on your birthday. That's a thing, I'm sure of it."

I wait. He waits. I don't think either of us knows what we're waiting for. Outside, we pass by the wooden sign with the big owl on it, wings spread, yellow eyes staring.

OWL NOOK SKI AREA

"We're here," I say. It feels like my body is breaking in half. "You never told me why you got on the bus today. Are you working?"

I want to say, *Can I have your number? Who are you, really? Please don't leave me.*

I bap the side of my own head as we pull toward the parking lot. My ears are ringing and it's getting louder. He's talking now and I can't tell what he's saying. I cough and my hearing comes back in a flash.

". . . walking around. Seemed like a nice day for it," he finishes.

"You're hiking?"

"Sure." He shrugs. "Needed a day away."

"Oh."

"And then I met you."

I perk up.

"And now I don't know what's going to happen, which is my favorite thing," he finishes.

"Interesting. Not knowing what's going to happen is my least favorite thing."

His eyes cloud over. "I get what you mean. Not knowing can go either way. Good or bad."

"Yes."

"The truth is we never know what's going to happen."

The doors to the bus slide open.

"We didn't really meet," I say. "I don't even know your name."

He looks like I've punched him. The air goes out of him and I see him struggling to regain his composure. He stands and so do I because that's what happens when the doors to a bus open. You get off. But I don't want to. Not yet.

"My name's Adam," he says, reaching across the aisle. Our hands touch.

"Blue," I say.

"Blue," he repeats.

My name is dessert in his mouth.

seven

Adam and I step off the bus like we're stepping into a picture on someone's phone or in someone's imagination. Sharp mountainside, the snow from last week's storm still fluffy since the valley's closed and it hasn't been skied flat and tough; bright blue sky, German-influenced buildings, wooden planks connecting them. It's rustic and so cute and sweet it's easy to forget the brutal ridges and traitorous rocks underneath. My parents had me on skis when I was two years old. That's easy to forget too, sometimes. How much I loved it. How much it felt like flying.

"It's so good to see you two together again," Rico says.

Together. *Again.*

I almost ask him what he means. Almost. But he's gotten out of the bus and is leaning against it now, lighting up a smoke with a silver Zippo.

He's not the one I want answers from, but still his words make all of me shake.

"Thanks, man," Adam says, like it makes any sense.

He nods his head at an angle that tells me I'm supposed to follow him. I don't have anything better to do. I have nowhere to go or to be. I haven't taken a step since getting off the bus. Frozen like a deer, surrounded by all this nature, I have the urge to sprint into the woods and disappear there, turn feral and forage off the land. Like I would survive a single second.

Adam turns around. "Are you coming?" he says a little impatiently, like I'm wasting time.

"Yeah." My voice comes out hoarse, like I've been screaming for days. "Okay."

I walk over to him, out of the way of the bus. Now he has sunglasses on and without access to his eyes, I find him opaque. The ski valley is empty except for some workers.

"Blue?"

"Yeah?"

"Hey," he says.

"Hey."

He's come very close. He could have maintained some distance but he didn't. There are only a couple of inches between us. I can't decide if it's too much or too little. I consider a step back but hold strong. He extends his hand again. I shake it even though we already met. Now it's his turn to freeze and I think maybe he will be the one to disappear into the woods, but instead he brings his second hand around, separates my fingers so they settle between his, so the pads of our hands press together. He tightens his grip and waits for my reaction.

Ever since I can remember I've been trying to figure out whether I believe in free will or fate, whether I think there's such a thing as God, and now I'm landing in the fate/God zone, because everything about this day and meeting him has been so fate-y. A thing like that should feel good but it doesn't. Meeting someone and immediately wanting to make out with them, to spend hours in a closet with them, wanting to know what will make them sweat and see their bedroom and meet their mom . . . this means danger. Wanting anything means it can be taken away. I would feel alone in it, except I know I'm not because he's here.

"What's happening?" I say to him.

He answers with a shrug.

We stare at each other for several seconds. "There's only a little snow on this trail. You want to walk?"

"You go on these trails often?" I ask.

"Yeah, sometimes. I like it up here even when I'm not boarding. It's quiet. I have a big family," he explains as we begin to walk. "Kids crawling all over me from dawn till dusk. My sister is everyone's princess. The boys never stop moving."

Sister. He has a sister. A shard of jealousy slices at me. "What's her name? Your sister?"

"Zinnia."

"Like the flower?"

"Yeah. Like that."

All the while we're walking upward and away from people and I'm kind of thinking about all the killers in the world. I could be strangled, raped, hit on the head, and left in the middle of the woods. Only Rico the bus driver would know I came up here with Adam. He would be my only hope for a witness. This is not something I would normally do, follow a stranger into the woods. I'm only five feet tall and I'm very aware of how small I am. I'm not upset by this. I have made myself invisible on occasion. I'm a cinch to carry.

He's at least six one. I remind myself I have pepper spray in my backpack.

I check my gut. Gran always says to listen to your gut.

I have a ping.

Keep going into the woods with the stranger.

That's my ping.

I hope I really did inherit psychic powers because it would be a real bad time for my gut to let me down.

We take some steps away from the restaurants and ski lifts, and pretty soon we're totally secluded and all I can hear is the sound of our breathing. I'm glad it's cool out. Or cool enough, especially when we walk in the shade near the Spanish moss–draped pines over the last of the snow.

"Are you okay?" he asks. He gives my hand a little squeeze and I take it out of his. Maybe I don't want fate.

"We're surrounded by ghosts," I say.

"What did you say?"

"That's how it feels up here. We're surrounded by ghosts. Like there's something in the woods. Something is watching us that I can't see from here."

He holds onto a branch like it's the only thing keeping him steady. He's breathing a little heavy and I don't think it's from the walk. "Shit, Blue," he says. "What happened to you?"

Eight

"Rico said he was glad to see us together again," I say. "*Again.*"
Adam doesn't say anything.

"And then you said, 'What did they do to you?' like you know me."

"Yeah."

"Do you know me? Do we know each other?"

He keeps going like I didn't say anything, then takes a sharp right into a copse of trees. I'm hot in the face and cold in the feet and suddenly I let out a loud yell, fists balled at my side. Birds flap from the trees and Adam looks up from where he's wiping some snow off a flat, gray rock.

"WHAT THE FUCK IS GOING ON?" I scream. It feels so good to replace the confused panic with anger. I scream again and birds scream back above us.

"Blue, dude!" Adam says. "Jesus, what? I'm doing everything you asked. What do you want from me?"

"I want you to tell me what the fuck is going on!" My chest is fit to explode. My heart is too big, my stomach is lurching like

I'm seasick, and I'm suddenly so mad at this person I just met. "What do you mean, what I asked? What does this mean?"

I'm sinking into the snow.

"Hey," he says, rushing over to me. "Hey, hey." He says it like he's hushing me, soothing me. I collapse into his chest. He catches me. "I hate those fucking people. They're butchers, not doctors."

"I can't remember anything," I say. "What people? What butchers?" I'm overwhelmed by fear, by anger, by panic. I'm going to die from this, right here in this clearing in the woods in the mountains. I'm going to fall over and never get back up.

"Okay that's not helping, Adam, you supreme twat." Adam mutters to himself, still holding me tightly.

I clutch him, my breath coming in tight spasms.

"Okay," he says again. "You can do this, Adam." He lets out a frustrated groan. "You don't remember me?" His voice rumbles against my ears. "You really don't?"

I shake my head, still unable to speak.

"But you remember something. You know you didn't just meet me today."

I do know that and my heart begins to slow its gallop. I release him a little. Nod.

"Okay, good." He's still holding me but now he's not holding me up. I can stand on my own. "What else do you know?"

"Just in general?" I say.

"Sure."

"My parents were ski bums," I say.

"Understatement," he offers.

"They never even had a real house until my Pop-pop died and left my mom some money to buy one." I search for more pieces of myself.

"And before they got the house?" he prods.

"Before that they lived and worked up here in the valley, stayed wherever they could, traveled to different ski areas and took me with them."

He releases me a little and I take a step back.

"I got used to traveling but I was also glad when we finally got the house on Tewa Court and I learned what it was like to be in one place for a whole school year. I don't know if my parents liked it though. I don't know if they liked finally feeling like grown-ups."

"Good," he says. "You all right?" Adam sits on the rock and pats the space next to him. "You want to sit down?"

I take in the long slab of granite and light up inside. I recognize it and this whole spot, but again I don't know why.

"Yeah." I still want to cry and kick and scream and understand, but I also just want to be where I am, right here next to Adam. All around us, nature turns up the volume. Birds get louder, the wind rushes through the trees, the sound of a brook in the distance doubles. Nature doesn't fuck around. This is a place for the truth.

"This is a nice spot." I'm overwhelmed enough by beauty that everything else falls away.

Adam looks up for a moment like he's searching for answers to questions written across the sky. "Yeah," he says. "It really is."

He worries, worries his fingers and then slowly reaches over and hooks an index finger through mine. I basically have no sensation anywhere else. It's like all my nerves have gathered there and the rest of me has emptied out. I wrap my arm through his and then lean over to kiss him because that's what feels like is supposed to happen next, like it's happened hundreds of times before.

"Wait." He pulls off his sunglasses and looks at me, searching.

I'm pinned by his attention on me, frozen in place.

"Your hair is gone because you shaved it off at prom." He rubs my fuzzy head. "You went to prom with me two weeks ago. You don't remember?"

I shake my head.

"In fact, we've done everything together for two years because we've been dating since the summer before you went into tenth grade." His voice begins to shake, whether with anger or nerves I'm not sure, and he's so close. We are only a breath away from each other. "Last week you walked into my pool with my sister's birthday cake. And you don't remember me because you had me Canceled from your memory three days ago. You thought we could start over," he says, "that we could have a clean slate. I guess it kind of went the way you thought. You still liked me right away on the bus. You said you would love me instantly again and maybe you were right about that. You followed me into the woods like you said you would. I always do what you want. But I don't think I can do this, not the way you wanted. That's not real, you know?"

I let this settle over me.

I know him.

I know I know him.

He looks like home.

"You were my *boyfriend?*"

"Yeah," he says. "We're together. Not just a little together. A *lot* together. You're my girl. Or you were." He slumps onto the rock as if under a great weight. "Blue, I didn't think you would actually do it. Cancel me." He smiles, sadly. "Together we eat the stars."

"We what?"

He gazes at me. "Never mind. I don't know what I was thinking, agreeing to this. I didn't want to. I feel like, if you want to erase everything we've been through you don't really want to be with me, you want to be with an idea of me."

"I was really really stupid three days ago," I murmur.

"Not stupid," he says. "Desperate. Sometimes we want to get away from ourselves so bad we'd do anything to get out of our own skin. I get it. I understand."

I turn and pull on his jacket.

"Adam."

"Yeah."

"I'm hella pissed I don't remember prom."

For a split second it's like he doesn't appreciate my attempt at a joke at all, like he might walk away from me. He doesn't though. Instead, our lips touch and he presses the middle of my back toward him.

I feel like an elevator falling up.

And it's this: knowing another person privately on a cellular level. It's knowing someone's shadowed parts, having known them for years. We feel the tragedies that are coming and the ones already passed and so we kiss harder and when we come apart we don't come apart, but remain there, with each other in that same way.

Something new is there now too, something besides fascination, curiosity, attraction, regret, confusion, even anger. Something that no longer only belongs to him but is shared, passed from his lips to mine like poisonous vapor: real, present fear.

And still, we cling to each other.

nine

After we have kissed and kissed some more, Adam and I sit there listening to everything around us, keeping our bodies touching, our hands held.

"We should get something to eat," he says. "Are you hungry?"

"A little," I say, realizing since we've been caught in this web I haven't had the chance to do any human things like drink water or pee or . . . My stomach grumbles mightily and we both crack up and we start heading back down the hill. It feels like we have forever to figure out the rest. We have a whole day. Adam is going to help me fix whatever is wrong with me.

As we come around the last bend back toward the parking lot I see Gran pacing around trying to make her phone work, which it doesn't here because no phones work in the valley.

"Shit," I say.

"What's Gran doing here?" Adam says.

"I don't know." I try not to jolt with surprise that he knows her but it does rattle me. More I don't remember. Layers and layers.

Gran's got big movie star sunglasses on, her nails and lips are red, and I can already tell she's cursing.

"Oh great." Adam looks across the parking lot from Gran.

"Who's that?" I ask, following Adam's gaze.

A small woman dressed all in white with her keys jangling in her hand is getting out of her car, gesturing wildly at Gran.

"You seriously don't remember my mother?" Adam says, darkening momentarily. Then he sighs and says, "Then I'm sorry for what's about to happen." He stops walking. "Don't listen to her, okay?"

"Your mom doesn't like me?"

The look on his face says it all.

"What did I do?"

"There isn't time for me to explain it and it isn't safe even if there was. You have to go find that doctor . . . Vargas. Actually, no. Find his assistant. Her name's Candy or something. Find both of them and make them undo this." He's gripping my hand and talking fast. Out of the corner of my eye I see Adam's mom spot us. "It's the only way we can put it all back together."

"Adam!" she yells. "Adam Isaiah Mendoza, what did I tell you? I told you to stay away from this evil freak-of-nature bullshit. You get down here right now!"

"I'm coming, Ma!" he says. "Calm down."

He gives me a fleeting, apologetic glance and then is rushing over to his mother, trying to intercept her before she can get to me.

"I told you if you did this you had to leave him alone. What's wrong with you?" Adam's mom looks like she wants to nail me to a cross. "You never listen to anyone. You do what you want and stomp on everyone who cares about you. No more. Stay away, you hear me?"

"Gloria, you leave her alone," Gran says. "How could you talk to her like that after what she's been through?"

I'm still frozen halfway up the hill, semi-terrified of this angry mom and not sure if I should come all the way down.

"Blue? Blue, honey? Are you okay?" Gran drops her phone into her bag and starts climbing the hill up to me. She's in her nursing shoes and they don't have the right amount of tread for climbing up hills, so she slips on a small rock and her ankle buckles. This snaps me to life.

"No, Gran, stop!" I say. "Don't come up here. I'm coming down!" But I watch Adam's mom for signs of lunging.

When I get to Gran she squeezes my shoulders, cups my cheeks. "Oh sweetheart, thank God."

"I'm fine." I bat her away. "What are you doing here?"

"When Turtle told me where you were I lost my mind. I threw myself."

When Gran throws herself it's a whole thing.

"I'm sorry. I know I shouldn't have skipped school but—"

"I don't care about that." Her eyes flicker to Adam. "I was afraid of this. Adam, honey, I'm very disappointed in you. We had an agreement."

"*You* had an agreement," he says. "I never agreed to anything. Anyway, it was Blue's idea."

"Don't you dare blame my kid. I told you that you can't do this! I told you it's totally insane and unethical!" Adam's mom explodes at Gran and I try to shield her. "They don't know what they're doing. We're supposed to be the responsible ones. We're supposed to steer our children in the right direction and what do you do? You let her do this stupid thing when she should have been in therapy, dealing with her life."

"We tried therapy! You know that." Gran yells. "I've had about enough of your shit, Gloria. This has not been an easy time."

"I loved Blue like she was my own!" Gloria shoots back. "But my son is my first priority, okay? He's made too many decisions that affect his future because of her, too many sacrifices."

"I didn't do that because of her," Adam says. "Why can't you listen to me? You never listen."

"You can't undo the past," Gloria says, pointing upward over my shoulder, dangerously close to Gran's nose. "It's not natural."

"It's cutting edge!" Gran bellows. It echoes through the parking lot, up into the trees.

"Geez, Gran," I say, trying to pull her away from Gloria, but she stands her ground, one fist planted on her hip. Then I look at Gloria and for some reason say, "Why would I do this?"

"I don't know!" she yells, then seems to realize she's yelling at me and I have no idea what's going on. She tries again. "This is some new fancy bullshit they're trying so kids will stop taking their own lives. They came here because of the bridge."

Angel Wing Bridge. I didn't remember until now, but people throw themselves off it all the time, and it's been getting worse. The whining noise goes full blast in my ear and I run to the closest tree and throw up into its roots.

"You see?" Gloria says. "Does that look any better than what she was going through before?"

"Oh you're *always* right, aren't you?" Gran calls over her shoulder as she hustles up the hill over to me. "Honey," she says. "Oh God, honey."

I'm holding onto the tree's bark, letting it scratch into my skin, hoping pain will bring me back to the moment.

"I'm going to take you home," Gloria says to Adam. "We're going to see your *tía* tonight. Your brothers and sister are there. We'll all be together and it'll be like this day never happened."

"Yeah," Adam mutters. "Sure. That's going to work great."

"Listen to me, son," Gloria says. "You're going to find someone right for you and when you do, it's not going to be like this, all full of drama. You're going to find someone you get along with who understands you and puts you first."

"You don't get it, Ma," he says.

"I do get it. Puppy love is powerful."

"That's not it."

I stand up straight now, so happy to find I can. Gloria goes over to her car and fishes some Kleenex out from somewhere. She marches over to me and hands it to me without saying anything. I wipe my mouth gratefully.

"I'm not trying to be a bitch. I swear I'm not," she says. "I just don't want to see Adam going around the same circle over and over again. It's time for him to get a fresh start too. Only he doesn't have to do some shit like you did and cancel you from his life. He can just walk away. He'll have a broken heart for a while, but it'll get better. And you? You don't remember anything anyway, so what do you have to lose? Let him go." She wipes at my cheek with her hand. "We've had some good times, me and you. Let's leave it at that."

"Adam," I say, but now my voice is no more than a whisper.

"No," Gloria says. "You have to do it on your own, without my boy."

I can breathe again, but I still feel so sick I stay glued to the tree.

"Nobody knows better than me how messed up it all was," Gloria says, directly to me. "The whole thing. A disaster. I feel for you. I really do. But enough is enough. You want to cancel something, cancel this. Cancel this morning and this day and everything that happened." She blows on her fingers. "Poof. Gone." She waits for this to sink in as a family heads to the trail using ski poles as walking sticks. "Get in the car, son," she says, without looking in Adam's direction. "We'll talk about this on the way home."

She turns on her heel and walks past Gran without saying a word. Adam looks like he doesn't know what to do. For a second I think he's going to run over to me and tell his mom to go away, but instead he follows her to the car and opens the passenger side.

"Blue," Adam calls.

"Yeah?" I manage.

He seems to want to say a lot of things, to have so much on the tip of his tongue. Instead, he says, "Remember me."

Gloria looks between us for several seconds before pursing her lips. "*Ai,*" Gloria says. "In the car, Adam."

Gran tries putting an arm around me but I shake it off. I'm mad at her and I'm not sure why.

They spit dirt as they go.

"Come on," Gran says. "Let's go home. We can watch some programs, eat some more cake, and I'll even call into the school for you. We still have time before I have to be at work. It can still be a birthday!"

Gran is just like me, or I'm just like her. When she's nervous and doesn't know what to say, she babbles. And that means she feels bad about something.

"How's your ankle?" I say roughly.

"Fine." She walks on it to prove it. "See?"

"Great, because I'm calling a circle of trust," I call behind me, as I head for her Oldsmobile.

"But—"

"Circle of trust! Now."

"Aw hell," Gran mutters.

It's as much of a circle as we can manage on a nearby park bench, but Eunice was in the car and now she's sitting between us, tail slapping against the bench. It feels wrong, like something is missing, like pieces of the puzzle are gone. Maybe that's all we are now, Gran and me. Missing pieces. There should be someone across from me, Mom and Dad nearby. Families should be polygons, not straight lines.

Gran lets out a tired sigh. She usually doesn't let herself sigh like that, but I see the way her shoulders slump, defeated; I see how her face sags and her lipstick creeps into any available wrinkle and crevice around her mouth. This is just another thing that didn't work to try to help me be happy, help me be satisfied and see life for the fun-ass romp it could be if I just relaxed, if I didn't take everything so seriously, if tragedy wasn't an unrelenting jackhammer.

Gran sighs again.

"Let it out," I say.

"Don't you give me lip," she says back and I'm relieved to see a little smile peeking out from behind the worry.

Gran should be lounging on a beach somewhere reading a book and sipping on a fruity cocktail. She should be traveling the US in an RV with her secret lover or doing her tour of important Civil Rights locations. She should be on Easy Street, not thinking about anything except herself and her own pleasures. She's earned that.

I make a pledge to be less exhausting, to be less of a burden.

"You want to call Daddy?" she asks. She still calls my father Daddy like I'm five.

"Does he know about this? About me erasing things?"

She looks down and to the left, a sure sign of guilt. "No. I'll tell him what we did now," she says, "about the Canceling procedure. It's only right he should know." She slaps the park bench. "Except everything's terrible now. I wanted to call him and give him good news about your mental health and I can't." She looks over at me. "I guess you're all in one piece. That's good-ish."

"Why should Daniel know anything?" I say, almost

under my breath. "He isn't here. Him knowing about problems I have doesn't make any sense. Let him have what he wants."

"What's that?"

"Not me."

Gran looks over to the creek, the babbling water, the way the sun glides its rays over its surface. "He doesn't get to just disappear. Not know what's happening with you."

"Because then you're the only one that does and it's all on you."

She snaps her mouth shut for a minute, then opens it again. "This is all Dr. Vargas's fault."

Dr. Vargas the mind eraser and his assistant Candy. Adam told me to find her, that maybe she could help. "Did you see how badly this was going to go?" I ask. "Did you get a ping about this one, Gran?"

"I didn't care." She says this with even more emotion than usual. "It got so scary. You were right at the edge, right there, and I wasn't sure I was going to be able to keep you from going over."

"Because of Adam?"

Gran takes a tissue from her purse and blots her upper lip. "Do you know you were the most independent baby? Your mom, she wanted to do everything herself. She wanted to be perfect for you. She never called me then, didn't want to share you. She wanted to do everything right and fix every mistake I ever made with her. When I came over she wouldn't let me hold you for more than a few minutes, like she was jealous of everyone who got to touch you, like she was afraid you would like them better than her." She pulls a protein bar from her purse as she speaks, unwraps it, breaks it in half, and hands me the smaller piece. "But she called me on your tenth day home, crying. You slept through the night. Your mom was half crazy thinking you had died, but it turned out not to be that at all. You were happy and content. You didn't wake up screaming, begging for milk or for attention. You never wanted to be held or to be soothed. You were just . . . you. She always felt you'd be fine without her."

I think about all the times my mother tried to be there for me that I waved her off or went into a bubble and didn't hear what she had said. That's why I don't remember whether or not she kissed me that last morning. I never paid much attention. We had our moments but they were few. It took her dying for me to know how important she was. Her love had always been a buffer I didn't even know was there.

Define privilege.

Having a mother who would do anything for you at any time and who always put her family first.

I was privileged.

"What does this have to do with anything?" Talking about my mother makes me feel a hundred things at once.

"It's been a surprise, that's all," Gran says, her Brooklyn accent thickening as it does when she gets upset. "You needing me. You needing my help. I wasn't equipped for it."

"Okay, let's get to it, Gina."

Gran raises an eyebrow. She hates it when I call her by her name.

"So I had some of my memories erased, which is not a thing," I say.

"It is a thing," Gran says. "In fact, it's taking Owl Nook by storm."

"What is it? Pills? Drilling into skulls?" I feel like I'm missing parts of my brain. "Gran," I lower my voice, "did you let them remove parts of my brain?" I feel around my skull for scars.

"Nothing like that," Gran says. "Although they do give you anesthesia while it's happening so you're really under and they don't have to worry about you."

"And people just do this?"

"Not everyone likes it but I think it's saved a lot of people."

"Like me?"

"Maybe."

I don't ask why. She's fussing with the contents of her bag and I can tell she wants to say things and is keeping herself from doing it. I have to wonder if I even want to know the truth, all of it. I'm not sure. I go for something I think will be safer.

"Why did we break up?" I ask. "Adam and me."

She looks up, eyebrows arched in surprise. "You really want to know, sweetheart? Really?"

"Yes."

"I don't know if you really ever did break up. I don't think you could. But you had gotten . . . erratic. You had to do something." Gran pulls a drink from her bag. "Vargas has a sliding scale. Something about research. We didn't have to pay much but that's why I've been working extra, which I shouldn't be doing because you need me right now. But I was scared. So many suicides."

"Angel Wing Bridge."

"I couldn't risk it. The man seemed like a miracle. He's written peer-reviewed papers. His story, how he got here, doing this work, it's really something."

It's all so improbable. "So what happens to me now? You tell me everything I erased and I go back to normal? And what about Adam?"

"Oh honey," Gran says. "You don't get your memories back. This is a one-way deal. And I'm not telling you shit, circle of trust or no. I'm not breaking your heart again. I won't do it so don't ask me. You're going to have to live with this. What was going to happen between you two? It was going to be over anyway. You're in high school. There's time to find your one and only."

"You and Pop-pop met in high school."

She seems to consider her nails before sniffing dismissively. "It was another time."

"The eighties? Come on, Gran."

"Another time," she insists.

I think of the way Adam's eyes crackled soft as the dying embers of a fire, of his last words to me. "He said to remember him."

"He's a kid," she says, like that's the end of the discussion.

I've been taken out of my own story and deposited back into it with pieces removed.

"Put Dr. Vargas and Adam out of your mind," she presses. "Don't try to change what's already happened. The last couple days you've been almost like your old self. You'll get there."

Suddenly I don't want the circle of trust anymore. I want

to be alone to think about Adam and a kiss, a memory I'll never part with willingly.

"I break the circle," I say.

Gran exhales deeply. "Thank Christ."

On the way home, Gran sings along with the Steve Miller Band and I settle back into the seat and think about what she said. Maybe I should try to accept everything that's happening to me, should try to move forward with a new life. Maybe the things I would discover about myself if I could remember everything would be so horrible I would want to die again and it would be an endless loop. I really don't know.

"It's not so easy, forgetting," Gran says, giving me a side-eye and sucking her teeth. "You should count yourself one of the lucky ones."

ten

As soon as Gran tells me not to find Dr. Vargas I know that's what I should do. It's the only next logical step. By the time we get home and Gran starts getting ready for work, singing along with an old Lizzo song, I'm on pins and needles waiting for her to go. I don't know why but I feel the need to hide my thoughts from her, which isn't easy with all her pings. She gives me multiple suspicious looks as I sit on the couch watching some matchmaking show, noisily munching on some crackers and complaining about how long it's going to take before Turtle and Jack are out of school and can come get me.

"Should I take the night off?" she asks, looking fresh and foxy in her favorite black scrubs, her lipstick in place, dewy with moisturizer, all the cracks and crevices smoothed over. "It's short notice but I could try. You know I was going to but you said you were going to Turtle's so I thought you'd be there and having a good time."

I leap up and go to the fridge for lemonade, chattering the

whole time. I'm being way too perky but Inside Blue is losing it again. "No! You go! It's just a few hours. I have Eunice. It's not your problem I'm codependent!"

Her purse sits open on top of the credenza as she loads in her work survival kit, which consists of Handi Wipes, Q-tips, breath mints, and a couple of Rescue patches in case she gets stressed out. She snaps the drawer shut and narrows her eyes. "You're not up to anything." It's not a question.

"Anything where?"

"Listen, honey," Gran says. "This is all a lot. I don't want to make light or for you to think I don't know it's a lot. Too much. I want you to be happy and safe. Can you take me at my word that you weren't either of those things?"

I nod.

"I need you to promise me you won't go poking around."

"I *won't.*"

"You don't know everything, you know, even at seventeen."

I don't know anything, Gran; that's the problem.

"No, I—" I say.

"Because in case you hadn't noticed, I'm just an old lady and you're just a poor kid. We don't have a lot of clout. You have to think, honey."

"I know."

"You don't know better than me." This is soft. "I know you think you do, but you don't."

"Yes, okay."

"Promise me." She hoists her purse onto her shoulder. "I need to know you're okay, that you're not doing anything stupid. Circle of trust–level promise."

I lean back against the pillow, grab my phone, and try to look as bored and annoyed as possible. "I'm not going to do anything," I lie.

She pauses in the doorway. "You're a pain in my ass," she says, "but you're all I have left. You need to be careful with you."

"You're a pain in my ass too."

"Yeah, yeah." She waits a few more seconds and I can tell by the way she can't get her feet to move that she's wrestling with her own intuition, not sure whether to believe me or not, thinking about that overtime check she's getting working extra nights and whether it's really worth it to take the risk and leave me behind when I'm apparently so unstable. I'm waiting for her to tell me she isn't going anywhere, that she's going to tie me to the couch or something.

That would be a problem because I need to go see Dr. Vargas *now*.

"Don't forget your toothbrush," she says finally.

"Toothbrush?"

She narrows her eyes as I realize my mistake. I try not to change my expression. "For the sleepover."

"Right. Of course. Why would I? Ew. Gross."

"Bye, Eunice, you good girl. Watch her!" She points at me and pats Eunice on the head and makes a tutting noise as she closes the door behind her and I go back to staring at the screen.

I wait until I'm sure she's not going to double back for her book or her powder or something, and then I sneak over to the window. Her blue Oldsmobile is already gone from the lot.

According to what I find online, Dr. Vargas's office is on the other side of town over by where Lacuna Industries has their campus, where old apartment buildings were torn down in favor of big glass structures whose constantly active TV screens you can see flashing from the outside. It's only two o'clock right now. If I hurry I can get there and back by the time I'm supposed to meet Turtle and Jack at five, but I text them anyway and tell them I'm not sure I'm going to make it, that it's been a truly bizarre day, and that I'll let them know later. They'll be there for open mic regardless, so as long as I tell them by eight, they won't call to alert the authorities.

I grab my stuff and head for the door. Eunice whines and I stop.

But Adam.

Adam.

All it takes is putting myself back in the clearing with him for everything else to disintegrate. I wonder where he is and what his mom is telling him about me. And then out of nowhere I'm back in that kiss, in the breathlessness that took me over. I want to be with him. The only way that's going to be possible is for me to understand what happened. If no one will tell me anything except that I was a mess, I'm going to have to go in search of it.

Adam, I'll remember you.

eleven

Right outside my apartment, my downstairs neighbors Enrique and Sasha are watching their twins pedal around on Hot Wheels and laughing at the way they're trying to beat each other through the parking lot. This reminds me there are still normal people living normal lives, although if I poked at their layers I'd probably find some hurt, something they're trying to forget, something they're living *over* instead of through.

"Hey girl," Sasha says to me. Her eyelashes are impossibly long and she has a tattoo of a naked lady on her bicep that looks incredibly cool on her.

"'Sup?" Enrique says, never taking his eye off his kids, his hands clasped and dangling between his knees as he sits on the stoop.

"Hey," I say.

I'm not sure how to tell them their mere existence comforts me, so I don't. I just wave. Donno, one of the twins, slides his Hot Wheels so hard he kicks up gravel.

"That's the move," I tell him.

Dr. Vargas's office is fifteen city blocks uptown. I don't want to take the bus. I've had enough of buses for today, and I don't want to take a Lyft because I only have ten dollars and I need it so I can buy coffee and a bagel at the Mountain later. Going from my neighborhood to uptown is a trip and is something I never do, mostly because I have no need to go uptown since my school is down here and uptown has its own high school, Del Norte, that has nothing to do with me.

As I walk, stores go from playing loud Latin music out their doors to nothing at all because their doors are closed so who even knows what's going on inside. It goes from dented-up cars to Mercedes and Lexus. It goes from panhandlers and catcallers to no residences, no one sitting on stoops watching kids play, no one asking for money because there are barely any pedestrians so it's a bad place to gather pocket change from strangers.

People pass me on bikes and one woman runs by in a pink bra and skintight workout pants, but other than that the street widens to four lanes and I'm on an endless path. When I finally reach swanky uptown I take in each business.

Fresh fish tacos and a selection of boutique wines; linens and dish towels I can see from the window are priced at over one hundred dollars a pop; a couple of clothing stores whose salespeople have asymmetrical, sharp haircuts and severely rouged cheeks. And of course, I think, of course their weed dispensary up here is three stories and has blacked-out windows and a security guard outside who looks like he's protecting the president.

I cross the street and there it is: a building made of glittering mirrored glass and metal, two stories.

TABULA RASA

I know what that means because we learned about it in English class. It's the Latin term for "clean slate" and refers to the theory that the content of our mind comes only from experience, that without it we are blank, in direct opposition to innatism, which holds that we're born knowing some things and with some of our nature already in place.

Gran said I came into this world independent, not wanting to be held or coddled. Some babies have to be touched all the time, so I already know the whole concept of tabula rasa is total bullshit. Still, if it was my innate nature to want to be left alone, the world has contorted me into something entirely different. Even looking at the words makes me feel lonely. I am not a clean slate. I am sliced up and flayed with multiple stab wounds.

I snort. It's an ugly noise. I would like to break this glass, to yell at this door and tell it that here I am bearing witness to the fact that there is no such thing as a clean slate and that this whole place is a lie.

I take a few breaths like my dad taught me to do when I get so feisty I can't see anymore and I say things I don't mean.

"Chill," he'd say. "Just chill, sweetheart."

I try very hard to chill.

I push through the door and cool, perfectly moderated air whooshes over my face. Rich people get perfectly moderated air. I get that. I'm instantly comfortable. It's probably easier to be in a good mood when the climate is perfect everywhere you go.

Inside the office is all white. There's a lobby with a coffee bar, an espresso maker, a lovely selection of teas (from here I can see mint, chamomile, Earl Grey, and oolong), a selection of Pellegrino sodas and plain Pellegrinos too. There are several baskets of granola bars, nuts, and pretzels. I'm too jittery for coffee but I go straight for the baskets, tucking several packages into my bag while people stare at me like they don't know what I'm doing. I don't know why they put these baskets here if no one touches them. That's a rich person thing too. They like to have options but not to need to take advantage of those options. The people in the lobby don't look at me for long. I stick out in my man pants and old velvet suit jacket. There are boxes of tissues everywhere, which makes sense. I put one of those in my bag too.

I walk up to the bright white counter with the security gate securely locked. I'm not scared or nervous or anything. I'm still pissed. I'm still trying to chill. Behind the counter, the office narrows into a hallway with a series of white doors. Pictures of people of every race and age with perfectly white teeth smile down at me from the walls. That makes me think of Adam and his white teeth and I have to push him out, hard.

Cards rest in a porcelain hand and say:

Tabula Rasa, Inc.
Memory Reconstructionist
Dr. Jeffrey Vargas, Ph.D., M.D., H.T., D.O.M.

On the wall behind the desk, a placard reads FEEL NO PAIN. You can't feel no pain. There's no such thing as no pain. There's only this, whatever this hellscape limbo is. I had heard that there were ways now to stop ourselves from feeling certain emotions. I knew medications like antidepressants had crossed over to a new level and that people, generally, are always trying not to feel because life would be so much easier to deal with without feelings that seem like they're always trying to kick you off balance. But I don't remember knowing anything like this exists.

So you forget that you can forget.

I'm mad about that too.

I'd like to ask for a manager and file a complaint.

While I'm waiting for some sort of front desk person to appear, I scan the people in the lobby. An old man sits on a white leather chair. He's holding a box. In the box I can see a few things, like a pair of gloves and a stack of letters. Is he trying to forget a wife? The one that got away? Something stupid he did? A few feet away a woman stares into the space in front of her, a picture of a small boy with freckles and brown hair clutched in her hands. I don't have to wonder about that. The old man is nicely dressed and his coat is cashmere. The woman has a very large diamond on one finger. You notice these things when you don't have very large diamonds.

Maybe when something puts a hole in your heart it's better if you can forget about it.

But also, it feels like someone came at me with an electric biscuit cutter and I don't know if that's a fair trade.

A woman/girl comes out of one of the hallway rooms,

closing the door softly behind her. She's a woman/girl because she's not quite either of those things but is more hovering in between. Maybe she's nineteen, maybe she's twenty-five. She's holding a clipboard in one hand and chewing on the end of a blue pen. Her hair's in a blond bob and she's physically frail in a way that's not so much a natural body type, but more a result of stress. Either way, she doesn't look very sure of herself, which is perfect.

When she sees me her mouth drops open and she murmurs a nearly inaudible *shit*. She pulls the pen out of her mouth and clears her throat. "Good afternoon, how may I help you?"

It's obvious she recognizes me.

I feel a slow pressure building. The room swims. I'm getting used to being nauseated but I still grope for the counter.

"Oh goodness, are you all right?" she asks.

"I need to see Dr. Vargas." I try to look steely and dangerous.

She doesn't seem intimidated, only looks down at her list and back up at me. "I'm sorry, that's not going to be possible." Her voice is practiced, striking just the right balance between soft and firm.

"What do you mean, not possible? Not possible now but maybe possible at a later time? Because I can come back in a couple hours if that's better. I need to see him."

She takes a tablet from the desk and presses some buttons. "In that case, the doctor is booked until August so we can make an appointment at that time. How's Tuesday the twenty-fifth at three thirty?"

"August?" My voice comes out much louder than I mean it to. "But it's May."

The man and woman in the lobby look up, ripped from their dazes.

"Yes," she says, in the kind of calm voice that makes me want to huck large objects across the room. "That's right. Three months. You're lucky. It's been as long as six. Shall I mark you down?"

"It's my birthday." This is a very stupid thing to say. I'm not five. Birthdays won't buy me favors at seventeen.

"Happy birthday," she says, like she doesn't wish me a happy birthday at all whatsoever.

"Let me see the doctor. Please. Five minutes. Something happened and . . ." I lean in. "If you don't let me see him I'm just going to hang out here eating all your snacks indefinitely until you change your mind or he comes out, whichever comes first."

"We could call security," she says, but it's like it's something she's just thought of and doesn't at all want to do and is perhaps not even authorized to do.

"That would be great for business," I say. "'Girl Loses Mind in Memory Clinic.' I can see the headline now. I bet the people in Washington would love to know you're experimenting on teenagers."

"I don't know anything about that." Her words are still clipped but the clean façade is shaken. "Where's your grandmother?"

"I knew you recognized me."

She shrugs. "I never said I didn't."

I hold my expression perfectly still. She tries to engage in a staring contest with me, which I'm very confident she'll lose because staring contests are Jack's favorite thing so I'm very experienced with them. Her phone rings and she lets it. Once, twice.

"Fine." She puts up one finger while she answers and makes an appointment for someone to ruin their life. They take the slot in August. "Stay here. I'll see if I can get someone for you."

"Dr. Vargas."

"Dr. Vargas is busy," she shoots back as she stands.

"Candy, then."

"Candy?" The woman's mouth twitches. "There's no one here by that name."

I shrug.

"Georgina," she calls over my shoulder.

The woman with the diamond comes suddenly to life. "Yes, Connie?" she says, hugging the picture to her chest.

"The doctor will be with you in a few moments." She points at me. "You stay here."

She disappears and I'm left in silence again, only vaguely absorbing the sounds of the flute-slash-harp playing in the background. When Connie comes back into view, a Black woman follows with braids piled high on her head. She's slim and even under her white and doctorly overcoat I can see she's built lean and sleek like an athlete. As Connie crosses through the gate to get Georgina from the lobby, the Black woman comes directly over to me, also clearly recognizing me.

"Hello, Blue," she says, with a voice like deep water.

There's a shimmer of recognition in me, a hint of something I can't latch onto. Knowing things is such a relief.

"I need to talk to someone about the way in which my eggs have been scrambled. And when I say eggs I mean brains."

The woman smiles at the edges of her mouth and extends a hand. "Dr. Erika Sweet," she says. "It's good to see you again."

"You too," I say, and I mean it.

Sweet, not Candy. Even Adam's mistakes are adorable. She gives me a look I can't quite read and then waves a greeting to the man in the lobby with the letters. "Hello, Archie. Paying us another visit?"

"'Fraid so," Archie responds.

"All right, we'll get you taken care of in a few minutes."

"No rush," he says. "I'm happy to have a little while longer with her. She really did have the nicest hands."

"I'll bet."

The smile falls off her face as she turns her attention back to me. "Come on," she says. "Follow me." She leads me down a hall, slides a card through a reader, and a green light goes on. She pushes on the door as it clicks open.

More white. Everywhere, blinding, blinding white. White cabinets, silver implements, an IV drip setup, and a table like when you go to a regular doctor, with fine white paper rolled over the top of it so each client gets a clean room, plus several chairs lined up against the wall, also white. The whole thing smells like bleach and lavender.

"Is this an exam room?" I ask.

"It is." The doctor is already busy doing things, but glances up at me. "You can sit there." She points to the table.

"No, thanks." I clutch myself.

She half smiles. "And why not?"

"I don't want you doing any zapping."

"Zapping?"

"Yeah. I'll sit here." I flop into one of the chairs against the wall.

She stops fiddling and sits across from me, taking her time, watching me carefully. "You wanted to see me, didn't you?"

"Yeah but not anywhere with straps." I point to the dangling white strips of cloth at the corners of the exam table.

"Those are never used."

"Still."

"Okay, so what can I do for you?"

Now that I'm here I'm stymied about what I mean to accomplish. "Can you answer some questions?"

"I can do my best."

"Why would I do this?" I can't imagine a scenario where everything about this place doesn't repulse me.

"Canceling is becoming more and more of a solution to some of the larger issues."

"Suicide," I say.

"Yes."

"Because it's an international epidemic."

"Yes."

"And parents would rather have scrambled-egg children than dead ones."

"Some, yes, although that's a bit of an oversimplification."

"And was I?" People have been telling me about my own sadness today. I wonder how bad it was and just how afraid Gran had to be to be in favor of something as stupid as this.

"Were you what?"

"Suicidal?" I let the word slice across my tongue.

"You were, yes."

"And who knew I did this?"

"Anyone who has close contact with you. We've gotten quite good at implanting blockers in cases where people don't follow the aftercare instructions, but most do. Most are as happy for the patient to forget as they themselves are."

"Turtle, Jack . . . everyone?"

She lays a gentle hand on my arm. "I know it's hard to understand right now and you may be experiencing some feelings of betrayal; however, you have to remember this is something you decided. No one forced you." Her face flickers with something—anger, maybe—before quickly returning to normal. "Now, can I please check your vitals? You're in a sensitive phase of the recovery process. I promise I won't do anything without your consent."

"No zippy zap?"

"No zippy zap, I promise."

I get up on the table. There's something about her that makes me trust her. It's not what Adam said either. I feel her goodness emanating from her.

Ping.

"Now lie down, please," she says.

I do. The paper crinkles under me.

She takes my blood pressure, listens to my heart, then puts a strip in my mouth. After a few moments, she pulls it out and looks at it.

"Just as I suspected. You're dehydrated. That's the worst thing to be during this process."

"Dehydrated?"

"Yes, proper hydration allows everything to flow and re-cover, allows your organs to process the memories and flush them out." She smiles. "You probably thought all your memories live in your brain."

"Where else?"

"Everywhere," she says. "That was our big breakthrough, what no one had figured out before us. Your very cells store your memories, your trauma, your hopes and fears and everything that has ever happened. We find the point of origin in the brain and then your cells have to release, your organs need to be cleared out. You should have been drinking lots of orange juice. The vitamin C, sugar, and water all work together." She peers at me. "You haven't been drinking your orange juice?"

"Well that explains that at least," I mutter.

I've only taken sips of water the last couple of days. I haven't wanted the orange juice people were offering me at all. Maybe that's been my body holding onto its memories.

"Now have I answered all your questions?" Dr. Sweet asks.

"No."

"I thought not. You're an inquisitive patient. I knew from the beginning."

"Is that bad?"

She shrugs. "It just is. I'll bring you a glass of orange juice."

I sit up. "No! I don't . . . I don't want that."

She puts her hands in the pockets of her lab coat and cocks her head to the side. "Dehydration is not an option. Would you prefer an IV?"

"I don't want anything that's going to make me forget or flush memories. I don't want to pee out my life."

For a second it looks like she's going to argue with me, but then she says, "There's that spirit." She checks behind herself reflexively then turns back to me. "Small sips of water won't do anything. I'll get you a glass of that. But I want you to promise me you're going to drink all of it. If you don't, you're going to get very sick." I grab her wrist and she removes my fingers, eyes trained on mine. "Don't worry," she says firmly. "You'll be fine." She presses a button on the door so a small light at the top turns green. "I'll be back with your water. I am sorry about this. If there was something pivotal you forgot to tell us, it could have given you access to a neural pathway we had shut down. We'll fix this."

"I'm not here to have you take away more memories." I will her to understand. "I'm here to get my memories back."

"Oh." She pauses in the hallway. Her shadow plays on the wall behind her, her reflection on the floor under her. "In that case we do have a problem."

"Why?"

"Because that is not something we do here."

"Never?" I ask.

"Never."

The door clicks behind her and I try to stave off the tide of desperation I feel. It can't be true. There has to be a way. I feel it. She didn't say it wasn't possible. There's a reason Adam told me to find her, I just have to get past the professional distance she has in place.

I lie there and think about all the things I don't know and

what they might be. I wonder if I Canceled political information or global information or fashion mistakes I made in fourth grade. I wonder how I picked and chose what could go and what got to stay. I really wonder, Blue, how you decided which pieces of yourself had enough value to keep and which you never liked and wanted to get rid of. And then you gave a man in a lab coat the power to sort your life into giveaway piles and bins for the dump.

The door cracks open just as I've reached the pinnacle of self-loathing and am about to start primal screaming.

"Here's some water," Dr. Sweet says.

I take the cup.

"I'll wait while you drink," she says.

Every drop is aloe on a burn. It's not enough but I don't ask for more. Her phone buzzes and she looks at the screen then back up at me. "I'm sorry, I'm going to have to leave you for just another minute. It's a busy day. I'll be right back. Don't go anywhere. I want to talk to you about something."

I can't just sit here anymore. A little look-see isn't going to bother anyone. As soon as she's gone I get the door open, wedge the white trash can into it so it can't close and lock from the outside, then get into the hall just as she disappears into a room down and to the left. I don't know what I mean to do. Snoop, I guess. Say I had to go to the bathroom. Anything but steep in that flat white.

The door Dr. Sweet went through is open enough of a crack that I can see inside. It would be obvious to anyone that I'm spying but I don't care. Connie is the only other person in the building that I've seen and she's plenty busy. Still, my heart beats fast and my hands curl into fists as thought getting ready to scrap.

The man who must be Dr. Vargas is sitting on a rolling leather chair, wheeling himself between screens. He has salt-and-pepper hair, done old-style with pomade so it glows under the light, and a moustache and glasses. He's thin with a small belly that sits like a punch bowl under his light blue shirt.

Across from him a middle-aged man lies at an angle on what looks like a dentist's chair. He's in a pink polo shirt, chinos, and very shiny shoes, which I notice because his feet are kicked up. He's also covered in colorful stickers that look like they have magnets in them or something. I don't know what they are because I don't know science, but it lands somewhere between absurd and impressive looking. What I can see of Dr. Vargas's screen is also red and yellow and green and blue. Another machine is spewing out a paper reading of something. All I see are jagged lines. The man's face is resting on what looks like the thing that takes X-rays of your teeth and it's rotating around his head very slowly with a grinding whir.

The man is speaking in a deadpan voice and doesn't notice us come in.

In front of Dr. Vargas is a Lego robot with wrenches for hands and a big white smile.

"We built it together," the man is saying. "She understood about Legos, about how they fit together, about their genius. She's the only one who ever has. Power doesn't buy you friends, you know? You think it's going to but then it doesn't."

Dr. Vargas looks from the robot to his computer to the

paper coming out of the machine, his face betraying no emotion at all. "Let's stick to the story," he says.

He is literally playing with someone's brain right now.

"We built it and then we went out," the man says.

"What kind of food did you eat?"

"Indian," the man says. "What does that have to do with anything?"

"Everything has to do with everything," Dr. Vargas says calmly. He continues looking at the screen but motions with his hand that the man should keep going.

"Lamb vindaloo," the man says glumly. "I always get lamb vindaloo even though it upsets my stomach. Naan helps. Lays a foundation."

"Got it." Dr. Vargas does something on the screen, inputs something into a separate computer. "Thanks. We can move on to the next memory now." He leans back. "Dr. Sweet? I thought you were leaving for the day."

"I'll be leaving soon, Doctor."

"Then you haven't changed your mind?"

"You texted that you wanted to see me?"

The man attached to the machine sighs and closes his eyes. The doctor doesn't seem to notice. He's focused on Dr. Sweet. Something's going on between them and I can't figure it out. The room is all filled up with the things they aren't saying.

"Yes, I did text you. Connie tells me the Owens girl is here. Why didn't you inform me immediately?"

I can only see a sliver of Dr. Sweet but she looks shocked, then smooths her face into neutral. She seems to do that a lot. "You were busy, Doctor."

"I'd like to speak with Blue Owens," he says.

"Doctor?"

"I'll see her as soon as I'm done here. Put her in the hall."

"The hall?"

"In the chairs. Let her work out some tension," he says.

"Doctor," Dr. Sweet says, "I don't think she wants to Cancel anything else. I think she'd like to undo it."

Dr. Vargas stops looking at his screens. He gets very quiet as though mulling every word in existence to find exactly the right ones. "We've discussed this," he says tersely. "We don't do that here."

"But there is a way—"

"There is *no* undoing," he repeats. "Now please go and get her and take her to the hall."

"Yes, Doctor." She looks as though she's going to do what he wants her to, obey him without any further argument, but then she pauses and trains her eyes on his back until he stops pushing buttons and looks her way again.

"I want to heal. That's what I came here to do. Not this."

"I'm sorry about earlier," he says. "But this is the way it is."

"I want to give pain back in a way that actually helps if that's what they want. They should have the choice." She looks so upset, the professional gone.

"Erika," the doctor says.

The Lego man is trying to crane his neck at them but he is secured in place.

She shakes her head. "Forget it. I'll go get her. I'll put her in the hall. But then this is over."

I run back to the waiting room with the feeling like she's

right behind me and pull the trash can back into its position in the corner, then let the door click shut. That was not at all smooth and there's basically no way she didn't see it but I pretend anyway and when she comes in she doesn't so much as give me an odd look. Both of us and everyone else, pretending, pretending, pretending. I can hardly breathe.

There's a way for me to get my memories back. That had to be what she was talking about. Adam must have known too.

"How are you holding up?" she says, all doctor again, no sign of her argument with Vargas.

"Fine, you know, taking in the scenery, exploring all the variations on blinding white." I want to scream at her to help me.

Dr. Sweet nearly smiles. "Good news, Blue. The doctor is going to see you and before that you get to sit in the pedicure chair."

"Pedicure chair, you say? Quite the full-service operation you've got going here, isn't it?"

She pats my knee. "It's all going to be okay, you'll see."

I don't want to talk to him. I don't trust him not to clamp me down into one of those contraptions and just go totally apeshit on my brain. He seems like one of those guys who thinks he's right about everything all the time when he's so obviously not. But her. For the second time today I do a thing I never do.

I trust my own gut and when she offers me her hand so I can get off the table I hold it and look her straight in the eyes.

"Heal me," I say.

She goes completely still, so still it's as though she's turned to stone. She takes a staccato inhale, then says, "I don't know what you're talking about."

She won't make eye contact with me again, and she leads me to a row of white leather massage chairs in the white hallway. Between each is a charging pod and a controller for the individual chair. Again, there are tissues everywhere. Lite Music plays in the background.

"That's it," she says. "Relax."

"As if," I say.

Only when the chair is digging into my back muscles do I realize I'm extremely sore.

I close my eyes. I can do this for a few minutes. Just a few minutes and I'll go back to dealing with this situation, with trying to make everything right. Making everything right is no small task. I am plain tuckered out.

The world drops from around me so the screen behind my eyes goes solid black.

A portal opens.

I jump through it.

Then I am there.

I'm on the little blue bus. I know that right away, even before I see Rico driving up front, see his less-frayed orange watch band as he reaches up for the big rearview mirror and makes an adjustment. My eyes are heavy and want to stay closed. I'm in a dream within a dream within a dream.

I'm aware that I have my head on someone's shoulder and that someone else has a head on mine. I feel the pressure of a skull and smell something sweet, like raspberries and milk. I turn to look at the person whose shoulder I'm leaning on and it's Adam. I'm not surprised by this or by the way my head fits snugly into the crook of his neck. He's angled himself for my comfort.

I feel completely safe.

I hear laughter coming from behind me. There are the little boys from the picture I found in my closet, three of them shoved into a single bench seat. They're laughing and poking at Adam who opens one eye like a sleeping lion and swats at them like they're cubs. My attention goes back to the space beside me, looking for the source of the pressure.

I feel the warmth of the body next to mine, the energy radiating from it.

I know its head only comes up to my shoulder, so whoever it is has a smaller body than me. Its hair smells like fruit. Its skin smells like soap. I go to touch it and it slips through space. There's no one on the seat beside me as far as I can see. There's only a white cutout of a person, like someone took scissors and removed the person from my view. I concentrate. This is not right. There is someone next to me, a warm body with warm body smells and warm body pressure.

I push against the empty space until I feel my hands pressing against cotton and behind it the solid, soft feeling of flesh and bone. It's warm. It's real.

My entire body gooses.

My throat seizes.

The portal is closing.

I jump again.

twelve

Right here," Dr. Sweet says as water slides up from my stomach out of my mouth into a trash can she's holding, leaving burn in its wake. "That's good."

"Blue!" It's Dr. Vargas's stern voice that brings me fully back to the present. I don't want to be in the present. I want to be in the past, because I know that's what it was. I was touching something, smelling something important. I want to be with that thing, not here in this lavender-infused nightmare.

Dr. Vargas is leaned over me, tapping me lightly on the cheek. He doesn't look worried. Annoyed is more like it. His face relaxes and he stands back as Dr. Sweet disappears the trash can I puked into. "How many fingers am I holding up?"

"Three," I say, and there's a slight slur to my own ears.

Dr. Sweet brings me a glass of water. "You have to drink. I'm sorry. I know what I gave you before just came up, but you need to. Take little ones." She looks at the doctor. "We gave her grandmother the aftercare packet. You'd think she didn't read it."

"She put four bottles of juice in my backpack," I croak. "I took them out. I didn't know why they were there."

"Are we back? Can we see? Are we over the nausea?" the doctor asks, sweeping a flashlight over my eyes, checking my pupils. "Follow my fingers."

I push the button so the kneading chair stops and the hallway is enveloped in silence. "I'm fine."

"Okay." Dr. Vargas drops so we're at eye level. "Let's cut to the chase then, yes?"

"Yes," I say, even though this body, this time, this moment feels much further away than the other. "Erika tells me you'd like to retrieve your memories."

"Yes," I say. "Yes, that's what I want."

"Well, I'm sorry to tell you firmly that there is no such thing. You purchased a one-way ticket here, which you were very aware of at the time, which you were happy about. You didn't want a loophole or any option that offered you the opportunity to retrieve what you wanted to let go of. That includes Adam Mendoza." He froths when he says Adam's name.

He rises so I see his nostrils hovering over me. It's comical. He looks stupid and I want to laugh at how stupid he looks but I can't. I wish Turtle and Jack were here. They would get it.

"I understand the emotional nature of these procedures and I also understand that memory residue is possible. The only solution is for you to allow me to go back in and scrape out what remains, flush your cells, that sort of thing. I need to go in and do a more thorough job." He turns his attention to Dr. Sweet. "We need to check across data and see if perhaps adolescents require a more thorough cleansing. We may need to make an adjustment, and we'll need to be sure to let your replacement know."

"Yes, Doctor," says Dr. Sweet.

"Scrape?" I say. "Flush?"

"Yes?" He says this like my questions are questionable.

"I don't want you to do that." I press the button so the seat goes back to its upright position. I think my legs will work if I try to get up but I'm not 100 percent sure.

"My work is important," he says.

"Yeah, but—"

"Do you understand what we're doing here? Do you understand the potential? People who would otherwise not be able to process their own pain are now functioning very nicely. Why, just last week I wiped an affair from a husband and his wife, and now they will go on and not remember a thing. Their lives will not be ruined, finances won't be compromised, children will remain unaffected. That's a small example. A *minor* example. One family saved." The doctor seems like an important man or at least like he thinks he's an important man. "For you the stakes were even higher. It was your *life* we were saving."

"I *know*."

"My point is that I'm sorry for what's happening to you, Blue."

He doesn't look sorry. Not one bit.

"If all had gone as planned," he goes on, "we would not be sitting here. I acknowledge you have been brave. You are on the frontier of something important, that can change the way we experience life. Your procedure can give us vital information about how to work with the adolescent brain, the teen way of thinking if you will."

I wonder if the doctor has ever Canceled anything of his own.

"Tell me what's happening right now," he says. "What is it you remember?"

"I remember . . . Adam, some things about him . . . and I don't know . . . a bus."

The doctor looks relieved. "That's all?" he says.

"Yes."

"That's all *so far*," Dr. Sweet says.

The doctor pats my knee. "Leave it as it is. Trust me. It's all for the best." He looks, for an instant, infinitely sad, oceans of sad, continents of sad. "What's done can't be undone."

The doctor pulls a pad and pen from his pocket, wedding ring glinting on his left hand. "I can write you a prescription, something to soothe you. It's too soon to tell what will come of this." He rips the prescription off the pad and passes it to me.

I look at the scrawl.

10 mg Alprazolam take every six hours as needed for anxiety.

"Otherwise I have only one thing to offer you, and that is the opportunity to put the Choose Your Own Adventurator on again."

"Choose Your Own what?"

"Adventurator. Something my son used to say. He'd say, 'Daddy, when I grow up I'm going to be an adventurator.'"

Dr. Sweet rests her palm on the back of his coat, the tension between them temporarily gone. He pats her hand gratefully.

"Kids, huh?" Dr. Vargas says. "They say the darndest things."

"I can't afford to pay—"

He waves me off. "It would be free of charge, of course. I can erase this day and any memory of me," the doctor goes on, "of Dr. Sweet—"

"Adam?"

"Naturally."

"No," I say again. "No more. I don't want anyone messing with my brain right now. It's okay. I'll figure it out. I feel better now."

"Yes, well, the choice is yours, of course. I recommend a minimum of thirty-two ounces of orange juice daily for the next three to five days. Try to finish drinking by seven so you're not up all night using the bathroom. Get lots of rest, no additional sugar or caffeine, and take those"—he taps the paper in my hand—"whenever you feel anxious or nauseated. They will help with both."

"Okay."

"I predict a few more days and you'll be right as rain."

"Okay," I say again, as though saying it over and over is going to make it true. "Okay. Okay. Okay."

But it's not true. Nothing is okay.

It's just another lie.

thirteen

Dr. Sweet leads me up from the chair, assures the doctor that she'll see me out. As we walk down the hall I whisper, "You can help me."

She's holding onto my elbow and she gives it a squeeze so hard I have to bite my lip to keep from squealing.

"You can help me," I insist. "I heard what you said to the doctor."

We're almost to the end of the hall now, to Connie, to the ringing phones and the unhappy rich people.

"I'm not like them." I beg her to understand, to somehow organically absorb what I'm trying to say to her. "Please help me."

It looks like she's going to deposit me on the other side of the white gate, into the light, outside, but at the last minute she makes a sharp right, taking a quick look behind her and in another minute she's pushed me through a hard-to-see door and has shoved me into a dark stairwell. She's breathing heavily, leaning against the door.

"I hate him so much sometimes," she says. "Then just when I think I can walk out of here forever, he brings up his dead son and I totally lose it." She growls. "The question is do you hate him enough to ruin your life, Erika Sweet? And are you going to let him manipulate you?"

When she sees me peering at her, as much as she can see me here in the dark, she starts as though she's forgotten I exist. But she hasn't forgotten I exist because I'm the reason she's here instead of doing whatever else she was supposed to be doing right now. We're only shadows as light pours from under the door.

"Tell me why you're different," she says. "Tell me why I should do anything for you."

"Because I won't survive without all of me." My voice is so certain a shiver shoots down my spine. "Because maybe you want to."

"It's not legal," she says.

I think she's about to open the door and let us back into the hallway then kick me out onto the curb, but instead she flicks on her cell phone flashlight and points it down the stairs, shines it in my face. "I told him not to mess with kids, but he does not listen."

"Men, amiright?" I say.

"You just be quiet," she says. "I have to think. I've never done it before. Not on anyone but myself. This is crazy. Crazy."

She's still undecided, hand just inches away from the knob. I have to turn her back my way.

"I want my pain back," I say into the near darkness. The light flickers from her trembling hand.

"What did you say?"

"I want my pain back." This time when I say it, I feel it everywhere at once.

She pauses, the light from the phone still blinding me so I can't see her. Everything is on hold, floating.

"Watch your step," she says. "Last thing we need now is a broken neck."

And for the first time in what seems like my whole life, I exhale.

Dr. Sweet leads me down another long basement hallway and then through several more doors. This place has a real underbelly vibe to it, like on procedural shows where they perform autopsies. Even so, I begin to relax.

"Jeffrey wants room to grow," she says as she unlocks door after door, and I picture rows of patients all hooked up to black box computers getting their memories sucked out of them. "He has big plans."

"Jeffrey?"

"Dr. Vargas."

Now we're in what looks like an overly sanitized locker room. It's much bigger than any of the waiting rooms I've seen and instead of having a patient's table and crash cart or a bunch of computers, it's covered floor to ceiling, end to end in lockers. Each one has a personalized code to unlock it that Dr. Sweet can control with an app on her phone. Inside each locker are blue vacuum-sealed plastic bags and sometimes boxes containing people's belongings. They consist of everything that might trigger memories, like the note and the picture did for me. These are called Remnants and before someone can Cancel someone or something, they have to get rid of all the Remnants in their possession. It's important for people to gather the items related to the Canceled situation because Remnants are powerful in terms of association.

She tells me there's a whole other room for furniture, large paintings, appliances . . . that sort of thing. Each locker also includes multiple tapes inside what looks like shoeboxes. In the shoeboxes are things like letters, movie tickets, memorabilia, all stored in small but sturdy manila envelopes, everything labeled to perfection. Dr. Sweet tells me all of this so I understand the system and know how I became a part of it. She doesn't pull out the blue bag with my name and serial number on it. She doesn't unseal the manila envelopes. She only slips the tape out of its plastic case and into a recorder/player and presses down on the rectangular gray button.

"Why tapes?" I say. "What's wrong with the cloud?"

"The cloud is not likely to be destroyed," she says. "It can't be made to disappear. Dr. Vargas likes that piece in his control. Analog all the way. Digital is in perpetuity. Now listen."

She says she wants me to hear my own voice and my own words from before. Not all of them. Only some. If I can hear myself and where I was coming from when the tape was recorded, why I thought this would be a good idea, it will help me make an informed decision.

"When I met you," she says, "you were one of the most miserable people. You looked like you wanted to eat yourself until you disappeared. I think you were trying to." She eyes me from the seat she's taken on the other side of the table.

"A few days ago?"

"No. You came in after that kid went off the bridge and Jeffrey decided marketing to teens was our next step."

"I don't remember."

"Of course not. We went when they had the rally to bring attention to the rising suicide rate. You said you were there. You've been trying to decide what you wanted to do for months. You had made an appointment, said if you didn't feel better by May fifteenth, you were coming in. And then you did."

"And now I'm back."

"Indeed."

"So if I go back I'll be that sad all over again?"

She laughs and it's throaty and clear, then gives me a look so severe and piercing I have to stare at the tape recorder and at her fingertips because I can't look at her directly.

"There's no going back," she says. "Please understand that before we do one more thing. You'll never again be who you were last week. You'll never again be who you are today. And you need to listen." She considers me another second and then goes to push down on the widest button.

"Wait," I say. "What if someone comes down here?"

"No one's coming. It's like an island of lost toys here. No one likes it but me, and I don't even know if I like it, but it's the only place around here to get any peace."

"Okay," I say, thinking of all that unpeaceful white up there. I can't quite lose the idea of someone bursting in on us, tying me to a bed.

There's a click as Dr. Sweet presses the button and the sounds of static, of tape running sloppily through the machine.

After a few seconds, the voices come, warped and warbled but recognizable.

DR. VARGAS
Tell me a little about why you've decided to Cancel your
boyfriend, in your own words. I'll be watching the computer
like before. You just talk away and I'll handle the rest.
Let's start with his name.

                                                        ME
                                        Adam Mendoza.

DR. VARGAS
Yes, Adam Mendoza. Good. So let's start with one reason,
hmm? What has he done to merit his own Cancellation?

                                                        ME
                                How long do you have?

DR. VARGAS
As long as you need.

GRAN
Go ahead, honey.

                                                        ME
                Everything I do hurts him and he keeps coming back.
                        He's like a dog on a leash, a puppet on a string,
                a man whose only country is a flaming heap of trash.
                                        That's me, by the way.

DR. VARGAS
No unnecessary flourishes, please.

        ME

I don't know . . . it's like we're addicted to each other instead of
being in love. And he's annoying and controlling and . . . I don't
know . . . every bad thing you can think of.

GRAN
Oh honey.

DR. VARGAS
Go on.

        ME

He won't go to college because of me even though he's
talented and got into one of the best schools in the country.

DR. VARGAS
Mmmhmmm.

        ME

We don't have any fun together anymore. Everything is heavy.
Everything is about death. And after what we did maybe it
should be. We shouldn't get a pass. It's like we're chained to
each other and not in a good way.

DR. VARGAS
I'm almost there. Keep talking. Doesn't matter about
what as long as it has to do with Adam. Just keep on.

                                          ME
                        Sometimes I hate him.

DR. VARGAS
Good, good. I'm seeing it now. Can you elaborate?

                                          ME
              I don't know how I can forget what happened and
                        remember him at the same time.

DR. VARGAS
(sounding distracted) Go on.

                                          ME
                        I need a clean slate.

DR. VARGAS
(triumphantly) Precisely. A tabula rasa. Innocence. A fresh start.

                                          ME
              I think it's either that or I'm going to end up hurting myself.
                        I can't—*(breath catches)*

GRAN
Honey, don't say that.

                                          ME
                        I don't want to know him anymore.

DR. VARGAS
Great! There it is! Let's change topics!

Dr. Sweet pauses the tape and watches me carefully. I don't want to show her how rattled I am. I don't like the lack of emotion, the pregnant sadness, the *weight* of all my words. But also, something about hearing myself talk like that gives me hope, because I knew when I saw Adam this morning. I *knew* he wasn't a stranger, that he was somehow linked into my own life. I followed him into the woods. I kissed him right away. And my body recognized him. There's no clean slate as long as we're in these bodies. We know what we know and when we don't know it anymore we know we've forgotten something. There is a sense of absence in negative space.

"Do you want me to stop it?" Dr. Sweet asks.

"No, I want to hear," I say. "Can I hold the machine?" I want it in my hands, this piece of me that is outside myself.

"Okay," Dr. Sweet says. She rolls forward and hands over the tape recorder, a clunky dinosaur of a thing. I sit there, watching it like it's going to bite me, like it's dangerous, which it sort of is. "What happens if the tapes get lost?"

Dr. Sweet shrugs. "Most aren't looking for their pasts." She rolls back over to her corner and watches me. "You know the clientele at this place?"

"I saw the people in the lobby when I came."

That seems like several lifetimes ago. It seems like I've been here in the halls of Tabula Rasa forever.

"Sometimes it's real serious, you know, why people come in here. The work Jeffrey's started to do with suicidal kids? That's something real. But the funny thing," she goes on, "is most of the time when people lose someone, a person, a child, or when they have something bad happen, if it's serious, they don't want to forget. They want to keep mourning so they don't. It gives them a way to connect to memories and touch whatever piece of that person is left." She makes a derisive noise. "Sadly, the bread and butter of this place is altogether different. It's small things. Something stupid someone said during a public speaking engagement. Someone farting in her yoga class, that sort of thing. It's the little things people can't face. We shut down small connections, Cancel the imperfections. Memory Botox. But you. You were different."

I'm leaning forward, every muscle tensed.

"Mmm, I knew you were going to be trouble. You were too ambivalent. And then Adam came in here, what was it . . . Monday? Was that only two days ago? That was your recovery day. He came in here making demands like you did today, insisted on seeing Dr. Vargas, all that. He made a ruckus and I let it slip that there might be a way. Moment of weakness."

"Or maybe you wanted him to know."

"Maybe. He banged out of here in a fury. He told me I would have to answer to God." She pauses. "To God."

Adam.

That explains the look of alarm on Connie's face when I came in. We've been trouble from the beginning, and when I say trouble I mean Adam and me, and how I love to be a "we" with him.

"I think Dr. Vargas might be reconsidering his idea of branching out into the world of teens. Seemed like a good market but it may be too much of a hassle," she says. "Too temperamental. Hard to control."

"Can I hear more?"

"Go ahead."

"Isn't it dangerous? That's what everyone's been saying."

"Only if a memory takes you unaware." I think back to being in that room in my apartment, not knowing what it was, the strange bed, the feeling like I was going to die if I took one more step.

DR. VARGAS

Tell me a little more about your relationship. The more specific you can be, the better.

ME

I don't know. When I met Adam I thought we would never be apart, that we would be together forever. Do you think people can be right for each other for a whole lifetime?

DR. VARGAS

(clears throat) Plenty of people stay married for their whole lifetimes.

ME

Plenty?

DR. VARGAS

Sure. I'm still married.

ME

But do you think people who stay together for a whole lifetime are still right for each other or are they just too old to get divorced?

DR. VARGAS

Let's stay on track here. I want to be careful about this Adam
business. This is a decision you've made without much
preparation. Are you sure?

                                                                                        ME

I, Blue Owens of Owl Nook, New Mexico, do hereby
swear on all I hold holy that I do not want to remember Adam
Mendoza or any of his siblings or his mother or any of them.
Make him go away. Take everything.

DR. VARGAS

Your turn, Mrs. Bellini.

GRAN

I, Gina Bellini, as guardian of Blue Owens, do hereby give per-
mission to Dr. Jeffrey Vargas to remove any memories associ-
ated with the Mendoza family.

                                                                                        ME

(after a pause) Yes. Now it's up to fate.

I click the machine off. "Fate? What does that mean?"

"We should go."

"I thought you said no one was going to come down here."

She's opened a compartment in the wall that has a safe behind its hidden doors.

"Whoa," I say.

"Before us there were jewelers renting this building. Safes everywhere." The light on the safe turns red and she punches it, then tries again. "I don't know what's happened to me. I have lost myself. I, Dr. Erika Sweet, have lost myself and now I'm telling all this to a kid, because I've realized the years of work I've put into this are garbage. Garbage that's just another way for rich white people to forget everything they've done that inconveniences them. And maybe Adam Mendoza is right. Maybe we will all have to answer for it."

"I'm sorry." I'm not sure what else there is to say.

The safe beeps and the door swings open. She grabs a pile of folders and shoves them into a blue bag she has waiting.

"What's that?" I ask.

"Insurance. Jeffrey isn't all unicorns and rainbows."

The room tilts.

I follow her back to the locker where she retrieves the blue bag with my stuff in it and hands it to me. "When I first started developing Eve, I was going to give her to the doctor for cases like these, because guess what? This is *going* to happen. Some people are going to want to reintegrate their memories. They're going to want something other than what he's offering. I thought we would do it together, that he would be so impressed with me. Your phone," she says, suddenly switching gears. "Text anyone who might come looking for you. Then turn it off. You won't be back until morning."

I shoot a text to Turtle and Jack about not being in the mood for a sleepover, then Gran to say have a good night. Then I turn off the phone. It turns cold instantly.

No maps, no locator, nothing. I am unfindable.

"We'll take the service elevator." At the door she looks back into the room, the concrete, the long hallway. "Fuck you and good night," she says, and then we walk outside, to where the sky is showing off all the blues of the deep ocean and the moon is on the rise. We were in there much longer than I thought.

It seems right to be doing this, walking into the darkness with the doctor. It's in the darkness that everything can be seen for what it really is.

fourteen

Dr. Sweet says the bag of Remnants will help me once I wake up but that seeing them now would only trigger a response like the one I had over the picture and the note and that it could muck up this whole process, but I still like holding it, knowing it exists.

The apartment is large and open with windows looking out on a clear, bright night. Owl Nook doesn't have much of a skyline. Other than Dr. Sweet's high-rise building, the only one taller is the courthouse, and she has a great view of the mountain.

In spite of how cool the apartment itself is, it almost looks like Dr. Sweet doesn't live here. There's a couch and a table and chairs, a chest in the corner, but otherwise no signs of life. No TV, no dishes on the counter, no cozy afghans tossed over couches. Nothing.

"This is going to take all night." Dr. Sweet wheels what looks like a massage table out of the closet and scoots it into the middle of the room, then plugs it into the wall. "It's heated," she says. "There are blankets in the chest over there. You can go ahead and grab those." She pulls out another case, this one black. "Here she is. Eve." She opens it and sitting in a bed of velvet is a crown-like device. It has small lights on it but other than that it doesn't attach to anything. It looks nothing like the clumsy, clunky thing in Dr. Vargas's office. It's charcoal-colored, sleek, smooth, minimalistic. She hits a switch on the device and lights roll awake across its side. It consists of several electrodes and a headband swathed in silk, and it looks like some fancy spa tool that will remove unwanted face flaps at the flip of a switch.

"Okay, you can lie down now," Dr. Sweet says. "Get the pillow too."

I'm crouched by a blanket chest that's filled with cashmere throws. I pull out a couple and a pillow and edge myself over to where Dr. Sweet has her computer open. She inserts a thumb drive into the port.

"Your mind map is on here." The screen lights up. "Do you want to see it?"

I nod and move closer to her.

There's my skull, my brain, with a series of lights glittered across it.

"Those are all the memories we shut down." She points to where the lights are duller than the rest.

"So you press a reverse button or something?" I ask. "Make them come back? Light them up?"

"I wake up neural pathways that are sleeping. It's delicate, complex. The brain is a wonder."

My body buzzes as I settle onto the massage table and pull a blanket over me.

Dr. Sweet is preparing a syringe.

"You keep all this stuff at your house?"

"I may have done some experimenting." She glances over. "I am not a perfect person."

"Has . . ." I hesitate. ". . . everyone survived?"

Her mouth nearly turns up at the corners but she doesn't look up. "I'm here, aren't I, and I'm the only patient so far."

She goes back to the syringe, taps it as she pushes liquid out of the needle. "I'm going to give you two shots. One is a mixture of a liquid that causes paralysis and openness, so the path is illuminated and you can't hurt yourself or me while going through reclamation." She glances over at me but is so preoccupied it's almost as though she isn't looking at me at all.

"And the second shot?"

"To make you sleep. You'll be out for several hours and then you'll need some time to get steady when you come to." Dr. Sweet sits at the edge of the bed and takes hold of my arm. "I want you to think of it like when we shut those memories down, we were drawing blood. Makes you woozy, sure, but you're okay. This is the equivalent of taking in new blood in large quantities. There is pressure. Your memories will come chronologically if everything goes as planned."

"There's a question?"

"There's always a question," she says. "This is the brain we're talking about."

"Will I see everything as it happens? I mean, will I know it's happening?"

"You will, but it won't seem like that to you. You'll hitch onto the most important things for you to remember and go from there. Like you're in a semi-lucid dream."

"But won't it be chaos?"

Dr. Sweet holds the syringe to the light. "You ever heard of *amor fati?*" She tap tap taps and doesn't wait for me to respond. "It's something I learned about in philosophy and then forgot, but lately it's been coming back to me."

"What is it?"

"The direct translation is 'love fate.' Nietzche said it was the formula for happiness."

I feel the tiniest prick as the needle pierces my skin.

"He said you have to love your fate, all aspects of it, good, bad, and ugly. You have to love everything that has ever happened in your life. You don't try to forget it. You embrace it, whatever it is, all the time."

I snort.

"Yeah," she says, "I think that's how I felt when I first learned about it too. But the older I get and the more I do this work, the more I think he's right. Who are we if we're fighting what is all the time? We're not in control. We're just so crazy we forget that sometimes."

Dr. Sweet smiles.

Amor fati. Love your fate.

I feel a second pinch.

"Life will hollow your bones and you have to learn to see the grace in it."

"What're you? A fortune cookie?" I slur, even to my own ears.

"Oh sure," she says, "make jokes." She leans down to my ear as my eyes begin to close. "Just remember, when you're in the belly of the wave, there is still a horizon. You just can't see it."

A wave of pleasure melts over me along with a trickling spark of a thought. I know I'm in for pain, for discomfort, for awful truths, but also . . . Also. "Dr. Sweet, am I going to get to fall in love with Adam all over again?"

"Have a nice ride," Dr. Sweet says, and then she and the room and everything that has happened today are gone.

i

Tatiana Tuttle moved to New Mexico from New York. No one calls her Tatiana, not even her mom. They call her Turtle.

I have never been to New York. I have been to a lot of other places to ski, but never there even though that's where Gran and Pop-pop are from. Gran doesn't get along with her family and says some things need to be left behind and Pop-pop does whatever Gran says.

People have not been very nice to Turtle since she got here. I sometimes don't understand them. They are mean even when she is trying to be good and make friends. It seems like the more someone wants to be your friend the more people are mean to them. Maybe especially in third grade.

What I know about Turtle so far is she wears dresses that button up the back and her shoes always match her dress and she clips bows into her hair. She's good at art and math and she sings louder than everyone else in choir.

Anno-ying. That's what the kids call her. They pull on her curls and say *Boing!*

I have never been nice to people who are not nice to me. That's why I'm mostly by myself too, and why Mom lets me take my phone to school so I don't have to be by myself doing nothing at recess. I read books on there and play games but I also watch what's happening around me even though I'm sneaky about it so people don't know.

Peter looks like the angels I saw in a church one time, white with brown curls and blue eyes, but Peter is not an angel. He doesn't leave Turtle alone. I asked my dad about it after school when Peter was pulling on Turtle's hair and he said people used to think that meant a boy liked a girl. But he said that's not really true and if he is bothering someone, even if she's not my friend, I should tell a teacher the next time it's happening.

So now I'm watching very carefully.

It's a pretty day and the sky is very blue. Christina and her followers are playing freeze tag in a circle. I am under the *portal* with my phone but I'm not really playing anything because I can see Peter as he leaves the game of freeze tag and goes over to where Turtle is swinging. Mrs. Bernal is watching the tag game and she is not seeing Peter going behind Turtle.

Turtle has her eyes closed and she is singing, going back and forth very slowly, kicking her feet on the wood chips, so she doesn't see Peter either.

I think about running to Mrs. Bernal because I know something bad is about to happen, but there isn't time. I put my phone down and can feel my heart beat very fast. And then I start to run just as he pulls Turtle off the back of the swing. She doesn't even fight or anything. I think it's because he takes her by surprise.

Then I take *him* by surprise.

He falls back into my arms and lets go of Turtle.

I hate the feeling of his body so I let him drop. He gets the wind knocked right out of him.

Turtle and I are in the principal's office. Most of the time when I have been in here it has been to talk about me leaving to go on a long vacation to ski, where Mom and Dad sign papers and stuff, or once about me not making enough friends. I don't like being in here for this.

I'm sitting between Mom and Turtle, and Turtle's mom and dad are on the other side of me. Peter is in there with his parents too. Everyone is yelling a lot because Peter got a bad bruise from falling and no one saw what happened and all the parents are mad about "lack of supervision" and Turtle's parents are mad because of bullying. It seems like no one can decide who was bullying who. They think maybe the bully is me.

Turtle is swinging her legs. She looks like she's somewhere else. I wonder if she's even hearing what they're talking about right now.

But then she says, "Thank you," still swinging her legs. She is saying it to me.

When the meeting is over, Turtle's mom asks my mom and dad if we want to come over for dinner. Turtle and I stand up and leave together. I think we're maybe friends now.

A hole opens up in the wall with flashing pinks and blues like the kaleidoscope I got in my stocking when I spin and spin it in circles. I can't see what's on the other side, but I step through it anyway, because like Mom says, I'm her adventure girl.

ii

It's a powder day, the kind where there's school but in Owl Nook there's an unspoken agreement that no one's expected to go because when there's good powder that takes precedence over everything else. My parents are on the bus up to the ski valley with me, which is not surprising. They've always told me school isn't where you get your education. Life is. They are "pro experience over classroom." The bus makes four stops. One in Old Town where Gran lives, one right by our house at the subdivisions, one at the top of the hill by the fancy houses, and one in the Owl Nook Ski Valley.

We bounce along and there's this excited feeling, people clutching hot chocolates and coffees, laughing and chatting. Twelve inches in one night doesn't happen every day and most of the tourists are gone after winter break. They'll be back this weekend, descend on the mountains like snow rodents but for today the mountain is ours alone. I'm already calculating how long it will take us to get to our lockers and get our skis and boards and get in line and trying to figure out which runs to do first. My parents always want to get to the peak before anyone else, while the snow is still pure and untouched.

My phone rings from my pocket.

TURTLE IS CALLING
TURTLE IS CALLING
TURTLE IS CALLING

She's pretty much the only person left who makes phone calls with any regularity. She says she can't interpret tone in texts, which is fair, but there's a lot of background noise on the bus. I answer though, because it's been a week since I talked to her. She's been sitting shiva for her grandmother so there's been a total communication blackout. Her mom's a little intense about . . . well . . . everything.

"Hi," I say. "You're back!"

"I am," she says. "We finally took the black off the mirrors this morning so I can plainly see what a total wreck I am. And now I'm at school and guess who's not."

We only have about five more minutes before I don't have any cell service. Once we pass the top of the hill and get into the mountains, we'll lose connection.

"Did you think I would be?" I say. "Did you even see how many inches we got?"

"No. You little ski bunny, you. I wish calling in to school because I want to sit at home under a pile of blankets and read a book was a thing."

Mom looks over at me questioningly.

Turtle, I mouth.

"Me too, T," I say.

"I don't know why you think it's okay to leave me like this."

"Hey, at least I'm not in Japan or something."

"True, true. But I'm still forlorn without you."

"You should try skiing."

"Oh, you're so witty, making such hilarious and endearing jokes," she says. "Call me when you get down. We'll do a sleepover. Masks, nails, the whole shebang. We can even watch *Moulin Rouge* if you're up for it." This is a favorite of both of ours. "My mom will allow it since she's kept me sequestered for an entire week."

There's a jostle on the bus and the conversation around me gets louder.

"I have to go. I'll talk to you later," I say.

"Sleepover!" she demands. "Promise."

"Promise."

"Oh! And I have to tell you about this person I met. They're so cool; you're going to love them. Their name's Jack."

"'They'?"

"Yes, they're non-binary."

That's when the door opens and a boy gets on the bus. He's tall, in work boots, with dark brown hair and warm, brown eyes. I immediately love the way he walks. It's like he was sprouted straight from the earth, like he's the earth itself. We're in the fancy part of town now, but he doesn't look like the other kids who come from this neighborhood. He's more laid-back.

"What's up, Rico?" he says to the bus driver.

The boy and Rico bump fists.

"Going up, my man?" Rico asks.

"You know it. All the way to the top." The boy doesn't have any skis, which means he's local and probably has them up there in a locker. He could also be a boarder. Either way, he's definitely a mountain guy because his reverse raccoon eyes from wearing goggles are seriously pronounced.

I wonder if we've ever been on this bus together before.

Rico laughs.

The boy scans the bus the way you do, lands on me and on the empty seat next to me. I have a theory about people who are good-looking like that, in a way everyone can agree on. Like, you could not have this boy in your line of sight and be like, oh that is not fun to look at. He just is. My theory is sometimes when a person is good-looking like that it's harder to tell what's underneath. You have to really pay attention to whatever else is going on and make sure they're the real deal. You can't allow yourself to be dizzy.

He sits next to me and his thigh rubs against mine and little zaps of nerves spike through me. I have never had this many consecutive thoughts about someone I'm seeing for the first time before. I've never had little zaps of nerves go buck wild in the center of my being this way either. He moves his thigh so we're not touching anymore. My parents, who are entirely oblivious to the lightning storm happening inside me, are talking to each other about what they're planning for the day, where we should eat lunch, all that stuff. I'm not part of that conversation and now I feel locked out of looking right or left. I stare directly ahead as the bus starts its ascent in earnest.

It feels like I'm falling or spinning or something.

"Hey," he says.

"Hey."

He's talking to me. I need to act normal. Sometimes when I'm nervous things go extremely awry.

"Those your parents?"

"Yeah."

"I figured. You look like your mom."

"Oh."

"Just . . . you resemble each other."

It's true, I guess. My mom with her black hair and white skin, with her eyes like black holes and her stupid long lashes.

I feel bad I made him self-conscious. He was just trying to be nice, have conversation because why not? It's a special day, a magical day.

"You ski?" I say.

"No. I board," he says. "I'm a total disappointment to my parents. They're both purists so when I started boarding they were like nooooooo, anything but that!"

This makes me laugh. My mom's a skier and my dad's a boarder and my life consists of them arguing over which is superior at all times. There didn't even used to be boarding allowed at Owl Nook Ski Valley. Renegade boarders used to go up there when it was closed and carve letters into the snow that said things like FREE OWL NOOK. They made T-shirts and everything until finally the valley opened up. People think skiing and boarding are for rich people, but not here. You can still get a pass for three hundred bucks if you can prove you're local. And there's reciprocity with a bunch of other places. That's how we do what we do, travel and stuff. It's not because my parents are rich.

"My dad and I used to go up together so I used to ski with him instead of boarding, but now he's sick so neither of my parents ski and they can't give me a hard time for what I do."

"Oh." I'm not sure what to say. I'm trying to think if anyone has ever just talked to me before out of nowhere. Not usually. I'm usually either invisible due to smallness and sheer force of will or I'm told I'm unapproachable. Hence the one good friend thing. Then it registers that the boy said his dad was sick. "Your dad has a cold?"

"Cancer," he says lightly. He doesn't look like it's light inside.

"Oh, I'm sorry."

"Me too. Anyway, skiing and chemo don't really go hand in hand."

"Oh."

"So you're missing school today?" he says.

"Yeah. You?" I say, trying to process the rapid change in topic.

"I'm in a hybrid school so we're off today anyway. I do a lot of traveling. Well, I *did*," he says. "I don't anymore. I used to go with my dad on tour." There's something a little boastful about the way he says it, like he's proud. It's transparent but also interesting. The more he talks the less high I feel from his physical proximity so I want him to keep doing it.

"Who's your dad?" I ask because his dad is obviously "someone."

He hesitates. "Arturo Mendoza."

Holy shit. Arturo Mendoza is the most famous person in Owl Nook. He's on TV all the time. He fills stadiums and Central Park and lives in Owl Nook so people will leave him alone. Paparazzi can't hold out in the middle of New Mexico. It's too boring and people can hole up on their personal compounds for months. Arturo Mendoza is not the kind of music I listen to but still, you'd have to be under a rock that's trapped under a glacier not to know who he is. You have never gone grocery shopping in your life without hearing one of his songs while trying to decide on your flavor of bagels.

"Yeah, that's pretty much everyone's reaction," the boy says, his smile tilted but open. "Thought I'd get it out of the way."

"Out of the way?"

"Yeah." He seems a little uncomfortable but mostly not. "I don't have anyone to board with today and I really don't want to be alone. So I was going to see if you want to take a couple of runs with me."

"We just met."

My dad is peering over Mom's shoulder with interest now.

"Actually we really didn't meet," he says. "My name is Adam."

"Blue," I say.

"Hey, Adam," my dad says, leaning over Mom. "Heard what you said about your dad. I'm real sorry to hear that."

"Yeah. I don't know what to do anymore." Adam sighs a little. It's an adorable sound. "Do I lead with cancer or not talk about it at all?"

"Got to talk," Dad says. "Don't keep your feelings bottled up."

Mom rolls her eyes at Dad. This is a constant source of irritation between them. Mom and all her feelings. Dad and his inability to deal with anything. And now he's preaching.

"I don't bottle anything," the boy says. "My dad made me beat drums in the woods in man circles from the time I was four. I should probably work on my bottling skills."

Dad lets out a genuine boisterous laugh. "Tag along with us today. We'd be happy to have you. I'm Danny."

"Dad!" Like this guy wants to come skiing with my entire family. Adam doesn't look as horrified as I would be if I were him.

"What?" Dad says. "Oh, we're not cool enough? We're too old or what?"

"Dad, ew!" I say. "Go back to having your own conversation. Thank you and goodbye."

"It's nice to meet you, Adam," Dad says. "Even if my daughter is ashamed of me in spite of the fact I'm definitely the coolest dad around. Except for yours, of course. He's pretty extra cool. And I really am so sorry to hear he's sick."

"Thank you," Adam says, his cheeks pinking up.

Dad turns and seems to be talking to the empty seat next to him. My eyes blur. I try to see who he's talking to. Mom laughs like there's someone on the other side of him and Adam cracks a smile too, like he heard something funny. No matter how hard I try to focus, I don't see anything except orange and white seats.

We go over a bump and everyone on the bus makes a *wheee* sound.

"This boy is special," Mom says, leaning over to whisper in my ear. "I have a ping."

The vortex opens in the side of the bus and I stand up, leave them there talking to each other, and I leap for the snow.

iii

A dark room.

I'm disoriented for at least a minute, standing in the doorway trying to figure out when and where I am. I hear the rumble of Adam's truck as he leaves my cul-de-sac. I am drunk or at least buzzed enough I'm having a lot of trouble maneuvering around in the dark.

My cul-de-sac.

222 Tewa Ct.

Owl Nook, NM 87212

Eunice's head pops up from between my parents' feet and she lets out a brief growl. She knows it's me, she's just annoyed that I interrupted her sleep.

I'm intoxicated by the smell of home as well as the small amount of tequila in my system. We were at Turtle's for my fifteenth birthday and she had a bottle. I didn't mean to get drunk but I'm such a lightweight that even though I only took a couple sips now I'm frozen, trying to understand what my house really smells like, how it can feel like my whole family filtered through a sense. Dog smell, sage, something citrus-like, old whiffs of palo santo. Nothing smells like this. Nothing will ever smell like it again. I want to bottle it, inject it, inhale it and store it in my lungs for later use.

The covers shift.

"Come here, baby," Mom says, her voice muffled by sleep and the sheets near her mouth. "You're creeping me out standing there like that. I thought you were a ghost or something."

"Sophia," Dad says to Mom. "What the fuck?"

"Shut up, Danny," she says. "It's Blue."

"Oh." He faces away from her.

Mom opens the blanket. I probably smell like alcohol and teen desire hormones or whatever, but I take off my pants and slide in next to her. Her body is warm and lean but squishes against my back. "You okay?" she whispers.

"Yeah."

"Anything I should know about?"

"No."

"Because if there is something I should know about, you know you could tell me."

"No."

"Well, did you have a good birthday?"

"Yeah."

"You were with Adam?"

"Yeah."

"And?"

"And what?"

"Did anything happen?"

"Why would anything happen?"

"I don't know. It seems like something is going to happen. You are spending a lot of time together."

"Yeah. Boys and girls can be friends without it being romantic."

"Not this boy and this girl. I think he loves you."

It thrills me to think Mom has some insight into the situation that I can't fathom. I'm just stuck watching everything Adam does lately, trying to analyze every look he gives me, pretending I'm not doing any of those things because apparently that's what boys like. Wanting something, someone this badly is exhausting in every way. I hope my mom is wise enough to see something clearly that I only suspect to be true.

"You think that because you had a ping," I say. "Sometimes pings are wrong. Adam and I are just friends."

Dad moans and shifts positions.

She sniffs the back of my neck. "I smell a lie," she says.

"I'm not lying." My tongue is thick in my mouth.

"You can't lie about love. I can smell it." She gets closer to my ear. "Tell me, when he gets near you do you feel like both ends of a magnet, like you want to get as close to him as you can and also get away?"

I don't answer but that's it exactly.

"Yeah," she says. "That's destiny letting you know you're in deep waters, that once you get in you won't be able to get out."

There are so many things I want to say right now. Mostly I want to beg her to tell me if Adam will ever see me as more than some girl he met on a bus, who he likes to play in the snow with and text late into the night.

"Were you safe?" Mom asks.

"I wasn't having *sex*."

"Not that," she says. "You looked in the back seat of Adam's truck before you got in?"

"We were two blocks away from here."

"Doesn't matter. Always check. And remember just because a stranger is good-looking doesn't mean he's not dangerous. You remember what I told you about Ted Bundy?" My mom seriously needs to stop watching true crime shows. She says it soothes her, but I think it also makes her paranoid.

"Mom—uch!"

"And I'm not pressuring you to be cis or straight or anything. You can love whoever you want."

"I'm leaving if you don't stop," I say. Ever since she met Jack, Mom is a veritable encyclopedia of sex and gender-related terminology.

"So are you going to tell him your feelings? Long summer ahead. Plenty of time for truth telling."

"It's not like that. I can't just . . . *say* things."

"Why not?"

"Because what if he doesn't feel the same way I do?"

What I want to say: because I would rather have him as a friend than not at all. Because life has been so much brighter since we met and because the electric volatility in me feels miserably good and if he's gone he will take it all with him.

"Ha! You admit you're into him!"

She tricked me. I sniffle with displeasure.

"If he doesn't feel the same way as you feel then he doesn't, and you get over it and move on with your life."

"I won't move on with my life. There's only one of him." I say this so passionately, the lump that is my father throws off the blankets.

"You ladies are killing me." Dad sits up. "Tee-hee-hee boys.' 'Lol we're just *friends.*' I have a river trip in the morning and I'm on store duty. We all know you love Adam. Go get him with my blessing, but first go to bed and let me sleep."

Dad has shifted from his winter gig teaching snowboarding to guiding raft trips now. This means he has to get up really early and go buy fried chicken, coleslaw, and chocolate-chip cookies from the grocery store so there's food for the tourists who go on the boats down the Rio Grande. "A little help? Some consideration? Can a daddy get some rest?"

I can't see much more than shadows in the dark, but his mouth is hanging open and his hair is scraggled all over the place and he looks like such a doofus Mom and I get hysterical. Like, it's so bad we're both crying from it and Dad's just getting more and more irritated so we try to laugh away from him. Mom curls herself into me tight like she can squeeze the hysteria into submission. She laughs into my hair and I laugh into the mattress and we try not to look at Dad because every time we do it starts up again. This almost never happens with Mom, this close physical contact, the two of us against him. It's usually

Dad and me, both of us with too many feelings to show. We usually both go quiet, try to turn the conversation away from emotions, and move on.

Dad is ruffled by lack of sleep though, and now gets up to pee and makes loud complaining noises about how he gets no respect in his own home and when he flushes the toilet and Mom reminds him to put the seat down, he has to go back into the bathroom like his spirit is completely broken. That's when we really go over the edge. Dad says there's a lack of testosterone in his life and even Eunice gets hella pissed, giving us looks like we should know better than to act so immature, and Mom and I keep holding each other now just crying, not laughing. At some point Dad stops grumping and joins in, laughing at how stupid and ridiculous everything is. Then we fall asleep together in a heap, exhausted from so much life at once.

I try to hold on to it, to them, but I can't because the vortex opens again and I fall out of my mother's arms and into a cloud of blue.

iv

I'm thinking about sex, trailing behind Adam and Turtle and Jack as we walk up to the Smith's grocery store to get snacks before we go to the city pool. It's hot as hell and none of us are in the mood for the tourists who will be at the river. Adam's the only one who can drive, although Jack just got their provisional license, so Adam's been taking us everywhere in his old truck. We have to sardine into the thing. It's a nice truck, a classic, but it's not practical.

So anyway, back to sex.

I'm not so much thinking about sex per se, like me having it, but I am thinking about the idea of sex, or why people want to have it, or why it's such an issue all the time. Like why do they teach us about it in school, but it's all about the diseases it can cause, when obviously adults have it regularly like a basic function and seem to really like it? We're about to be in tenth grade. I hope they start telling us the truth about love and sex and all the rest of it because there are things I'd like to know.

I know my parents still have sex sometimes, even though they argue a lot, because it's the only time they close and lock their door and I know it consists of more than STDs and possible pregnancy, and I did really enjoy making out in the closet a couple months ago, but I've been dreaming about Adam and we're just friends so the whole thing is a disaster. I can't even act normal around him anymore, if I ever could.

And it's not like I want to have sex with him right away or something. But I would like to kiss him. Very much I would like that. I wouldn't mind running my hands over the skin under his shirt, feeling his breath on my neck, his fingertips on my belly. I can't even talk to Turtle about how badly my brain has been hijacked by Adam because she's so loopy over Jack there's no room for me to neurotically text her about whether or not he likes me. I'm too busy doing that for her, even though Jack has landed in Turtle's life in a way that feels permanent and I don't think T has anything to worry about.

It's hot in the parking lot in July, but not as hot as it was in the truck, which doesn't have AC. Turtle complains about it a lot, but I don't care at all. I get to squeeze into Adam, our sweat combining in a way that feels personal.

Something has happened to my thoughts. Suddenly a lot of people seem highly attractive. Girls, boys. There's this whole rustling, bustling thing going on and sometimes all I can think about is all the beautiful I see on the streets. In fact, lately, everyone seems a little bit beautiful, even the lady at the store with no teeth and a moustache whose stockings bunch at the knees. It's her eyes. All the shapes and colors excite me. People I don't know, in bright and bold fashion, send me into fits of joy. Boys who have been in the most awful of awkward phases have suddenly become themselves. And as for me, even though I remain small, I can see my jawline has stabilized, my lips have poofed, my eye shape has widened, and my breasts, bitty as they are, have taken on a pleasing shape and push against the front of my T-shirt.

I think I've fallen in love with the whole world, but Adam most of all.

Adam says his therapist told him he trauma-bonded to me because I met him right when his dad started his cancer treatments. I wonder if that's why he friend-zoned me so hard. Also, I would like to slap his therapist. Maybe we just liked each other right away. Sometimes you just know when a person is supposed to be in your life, like with me and Turtle, or now Turtle and Jack. Jack and Turtle have been attached at the face since February and now that Adam and I hang out with them all the time, we're basically their kissy-face audience. Even though that part can sometimes be a bummer, I feel like we were all always supposed to be together, like something has clicked with all of us as a group.

I think Adam might love me and that Mom may not have been wrong about that. We are together almost every day. I went clothes shopping with him and picked out some of his T-shirts. He reads a lot and has given me books and we've spent all summer so far lying around, reading, sometimes even poetry, which seemed so unlikely at first. I told him it seems like poetry answers questions I didn't know I had, and he stared at me for a full minute before he went on reading. I thought that cheesy behavior such as reading poetry out loud would make me want to projectile, but it doesn't. It makes me want to leap with him. It makes me feel like we understand the same things.

I've come to understand that almost everything he does is an attempt to reach out to his dad. He reads poetry, likes to camp in the woods alone, listens to music and plays his guitar all the time, and basically never gives up an opportunity for adventure, and it's all because those are things his dad taught him and right now that's all he has.

I'm not paying attention to where I'm going because I'm so busy having all these thoughts and I topple off the sidewalk and my ankle twists. I'm always hurting my ankle. It's like the doctor told me last time I sprained it, once you break your ankle one time, you're always going to have to look out for it. I don't want to cry out. That's the last thing I want, but it really does hurt, and it sends sharp bursts of pain through my foot and up the side of my leg.

"You okay?" Turtle crouches down beside me.

"Can you stand up?" Adam asks.

I try but a burn flies up my leg and I buckle right back onto the sidewalk. I haven't been embarrassed about anything today, even walking beside Adam, feeling heated every time we talk, feeling the crushing weight of everything we aren't saying to each other, our interest in each other a stiletto heel of a question—until right this second.

Now it's like omgomg whyyyyyy did he have to be here to see me fall?

Uch.

"Hold on, I have an idea." Adam disappears behind the sliding doors, into Smith's.

Turtle turns to me with a knowing look as soon as he's gone. "He likes you and you like him and you guys are going to do it."

Once again I heat at the thought of all the things happening in my head occurring in real life. "He doesn't like me that way." I want to be corrected, to be told that he does absolutely like me that way, but Jack only scoots onto the sidewalk and pulls out their phone.

"Have you even talked to him about it? I'd say you're being exceedingly weeny-ish. It's the thing that worries me about you the most, B. You have to learn to talk about your feelings. It's the only way you get to any of the good stuff." Turtle sits down next to me.

"He says we trauma bonded," I admit.

"What does that even mean? The entire universe is one big trauma bonded together via other trauma. What else would you call the Big Bang? Life is basically nothing but trauma so how else are you supposed to bond to someone? Look at childbirth! Moms go through all the pain and stress and pregnancy and everything and then they have the baby and are instantly more bonded than they are to anything else in existence. Are you going to tell me that's not trauma bonding?"

Jack smiles.

"Turtle." I suck in my breath as another pain shoots over my foot and leg. "Stop talking about this. Also, I'm literally perishing from ankle discomfort."

She takes a beat. "Well anyway, please make out." Turtle glances at my foot, instantly pales, and puts a hand up to shield her eyes. "Also, your ankle is gross."

I look. It's beginning to puff out and bruise.

Adam reappears with something in hand. Every time I see him it's like I'm being shocked with a cattle prod, like I'm never going to get used to looking at him.

He crouches down. "Are you okay?"

I try not to stare at his excellent face. "It hurts. I don't think I can walk on it."

"Yeah, no. Don't even try it." He puts something cool against my ankle. "I got you ice."

Behind him, Turtle and Jack look at each other, then at me. Turtle raises her eyebrows.

"This will make the swelling go down," he says.

"Thanks," I say. "I've broken it before, in karate class. I think this is just a sprain."

"We should go get it checked out." He looks up at me and a piece of hair falls across his eyes. "Also, can we discuss your karate history?"

"What's to discuss? It was brief and ended with a broken ankle."

"I see."

My stomach does ten perfectly landed backflips.

"We were supposed to get snacks and go to the pool," I say.

"We can go to the pool after we get this checked out. They're probably at least going to want to stabilize it."

"The clinic takes forever. I'm completely fine. I can have my grandma deal with it when she gets off work."

"Does you grandma have an X-ray machine? No? Didn't think so."

"It looks like someone implanted a melon where your ankle was," Turtle says.

She's not wrong. It's getting worse by the second.

"Urgent Care is a block away. We have all afternoon. Hold that there," he says, pointing to the ice pack. He throws Jack his keys. "We'll meet you at the pool. Make sure you get Oreos for Blue."

He remembered my favorite snack.

"I only have my permit," Jack says.

"It's okay," Adam says.

"Anything I should know about your truck before I attempt to drive it?"

"Yeah, don't wreck it."

"Oh thanks," Jack drawls.

He reaches over and for a second I'm not sure what he's doing. It almost seems like he might be coming in for a kiss, but then he scoops me up easily. My heart picks up speed, mouth aggressively dry. We're so close. So face-to-face.

"Fine. We'll meet you at the pool in your entirely unwrecked truck," Jack says. "I hope."

"Not that anyone cares," Turtle says.

Adam carries me over to Urgent Care. He says he brought his brother Miguel to the Old Town park once and he fell off the slide so he knows it's only a block away.

We never talk about his house at the top of the hill, or his brothers and sister, or the pool and tennis court I know he has in his yard because I've seen pictures of it on *E! News*, but I do notice how he says he came down to Old Town like he's descended from somewhere up on high.

I should be thinking about the pain I'm in but I don't really feel it now that it's numb from ice and endorphins. He's strong and carrying me and I should be focusing on that too. Instead I'm focused on being this close to him, his humanness and flaws. He has pores and hairs sticking out of his cheek and he's a little smelly from being out in the heat all day. It's not a bad smell but it's there. It's good to remind myself he isn't superhuman and he's just a boy like all the other boys.

The difference is he feels like *my* boy.

He sets me down on the bench at Urgent Care. There aren't that many people in the place, which is good. The air-conditioning doesn't seem to work, which is bad. He brings me the paperwork and I fill out the information.

While we're waiting I tell Adam how I broke my ankle the first time in karate class when I kicked the wood at the wrong angle, and how my dad thought I was exaggerating about the pain and made me finish class; how it was Mom who noticed how swollen it was and dashed me to the ER.

"You don't tell me stuff about you very often," he says. "I like hearing about your life."

"You don't tell me about you either," I counter.

"I would. I usually do." He darkens like someone switched off a lamp. "It's just life's all kinds of fucked up right now."

"Yeah."

"You want me to tell you about how my dad can't get out of bed anymore?"

"No. I mean yeah. You can talk about whatever. I'll listen."

"You've never had to deal with something like this."

"Like your dad?"

"Yeah. It makes you pay attention to everything, want to be nice to everyone because you never know what someone is going through. Makes you mad too though. At them, sometimes. At the person who is sick; at everyone whose dad isn't sick."

"Yeah." He's right. I really don't know what he's going through and I have the sense I'm somehow unexcavated, like a piece of land with dinosaur bones underneath that haven't been found yet. Pop-pop died a couple years ago and that totally sucked but it didn't feel like he was getting ripped away from everyone before his time. It felt more like he was meant to go right then and we were all sad and cried and everything, but it was okay. Everyone dies. That's a thing. But my dad. I can't imagine what it would be like to have him die. Not now. I would die too. "I'm really sorry."

Adam glances around the doctor's office. We're surrounded by people who are probably listening to us and everything we're saying, but it feels like Adam and I are separate from them, protected.

"You've been to my house," I say.

"Yeah."

"I haven't been to yours."

"You don't want to go there right now."

"I'm just saying it's not just me who doesn't talk about things. Sometimes it's just easier to do stuff."

"Yeah." He's looking at me very intensely and I am not looking away.

I could not be more self-conscious right now if I were completely naked in this doctor's office, especially because all I want to do is say *I love you I love you I love you* like it's a mantra until we both vibrate with the truth of it, until he says it back and lets me hold him the way I want to. I have never wanted to hold someone before, to show them all my love with the space between my arms.

"Blue Owens," a nurse calls from the doorway.

Adam helps me over to her.

The vortex appears behind the nurse.

"I can walk alone," I say to him.

"You sure?"

I'm watching the swirling in the hallway and all the pretty colors.

"Yeah." I take one last look at him, his hopeful, sad eyes, him holding the clipboard with my paperwork.

I hobble through.

v

I wake up at a picnic. I've been napping with a hat over my face.

My phone buzzes next to me. I can feel it's Adam.

After we left Urgent Care yesterday with my foot in a boot, we went to the pool but instead of hanging out with Turtle and Jack, we kept to ourselves under a tree in the shade and we talked. Even though I didn't tell him how I felt about him, or us, I did tell him other things: that I'm worried about my parents now, that death terrifies me and I spend nights staring at my ceiling imagining myself rotting and full of worms and I just can't help it; that the way feelings come in and take over when I should be able to think clearly scares me more than anything else. Because what happens when I'm completely consumed? What then?

Then I went home and googled him. I can't believe I hadn't thought to do that before. I was too focused on stalking his dad. I found a picture of him, a little boy banging a drum onstage, tucked into his mom's arms. I always feel like I've gotten to go more places than a lot of people because of how my parents have to ski every mountain, but he's really been everywhere on earth.

Arturo seems like a good dad, although you never can tell from social media. It's all tennis courts and oceans and feasts and throngs of adoring fans. He favors white or cream cotton peasant shirts, casual, easy black cotton pants. He looks strong, muscular, which is so different from that picture in his hospital bed. I'm trash for looking but I can't help it. I want to know everything there is to know about Adam. I want to assimilate his essence.

Right now we're up really high in the mountains and the sky is a bright, unrelenting blue. Jack wanted to get out of the city and their parents let them have the car because they don't care about things like learner's permits and driving Adam's truck made Jack brave, so we drove out of town and deep into the mountains, not to a hiking trail but up and out.

No one comes up here so the grass is like up to my waist except where it's been trampled by animals. There are bears and mountain lions, sometimes rams or elk, but I'm counting on them wanting to stay far away from us. We've nestled ourselves on a couple of flat rocks. The hissing trees as the wind passes through leaves reminds me of Adam and water and lapping, lazy waves. Everything reminds me of Adam. I don't have control over my thoughts or feelings at all whatsoever anymore.

I'll be walking across a parking lot and all of a sudden I'm doubled over with a memory of something sweet Adam's done or something he probably didn't even know was miraculous or some goofy comment he made and I can't even breathe. Everything seizes at once. I'll stay like that for thirty seconds or something and then *bloop* it's gone and I can walk again. I have to place my hand on my lower belly to still everything and then all that's left is residue. I float on that residue.

We're all in our underwear, me, Turtle, and Jack. Getting almost naked in the secluded wilderness is something we wouldn't normally do because of creepy dudes, but since school starts the second week of August, it feels like summer's almost over and we're feeling less cautious than usual. When it's gone it will be winter until May. That's how it is. Summer hangs on until the end of September, sometimes there are hot days into October, and then it's snowing and bitter and windy and that's that until it's May again.

"What are you guys most excited about this year?" I say from inside my hat.

"Show choir," they both say.

I'm looking forward to a fun year at school. I even made Mom and Dad promise to leave me with Gran this year when they go on their ski trip instead of yanking me out like they usually do. I want to see how it feels to have a whole year in school like everyone else. Also, I don't want to leave Adam. Not now, since his father is fading out, but really not ever.

"You should join," Turtle says.

"Show choir? No," I say. Then, "No way."

"Why not?" Turtle whines. "You'd get to be with us and your voice is so good."

"I can't dance. Not like that. I won't. You guys go ahead. You'll rock it. It will be great."

"My nipples are burning," Jack says. "Throw me that sunblock."

The vortex sucks me through my hat and spits me out and into the night that changed everything.

I can hardly wait.

vi

We're at a party at a house in Adam's neighborhood so I shouldn't be surprised when he walks in, but I am. I've learned that he's friends with a lot of people and talks easily with almost everyone. Look at how he started the conversation with me on the bus. If he hadn't done that I don't know where I'd be now. I don't know *who* I'd be.

He looks *adorable* tonight: T-shirt I picked out, hair kind of flopping around, amazing shoes.

We're not a couple or anything but I still feel like I should have told him I was going to be here and he should have told me, but there are no messages from him on my phone. We're in an odd place. I should go give him a hug or something. I see him see me and he raises a hand in greeting but doesn't come over to me. I hate everything about this except how attractive he is. Maybe I hate that too.

"More beer," I say, and Jack and Turtle give each other one of their looks.

Jack doesn't drink and never has. Their mom is an alcoholic and they say it's rampant in their family so they don't want to take any risks. Also they say it pollutes their spirit. Right now the level of anxiety it's giving me being in Adam's presence is stressful on a soul level so I don't mind being polluted.

God, Adam is so amazing.

"Gin," I say. "Make it gin."

Turtle charges over to the keg-slash-bar, because this house is swanky enough to have such a setup, even if said alcohol is being presided over by boys.

"Okay, honey," Jack says, when Turtle's gone. "You seriously need to get it together. You're a queen. Got to act like one."

"Not everyone is smooth like you."

"*Pfhth.*" The noise Jack makes is like what I said is totally ridiculous. Maybe they don't know that they glide everywhere. Maybe there are lots of things we don't know about ourselves. The thought of this is unsettling.

I don't feel like a queen. I feel every inch of my five-foot-zero stature and no more. "I hate that Turtle skipped a grade. We never get to be in class together." I've been griping about this a lot, especially when I'm thinking about Adam and want to turn the focus to something else.

I think Jack's about to scoff but they don't. Instead they say,

"Yeah, I guess so. We'll see you between classes. We'll put in a request for lockers close to each other again. You won't be alone."

Even though I'm actively complaining about something that does bother me sometimes, it's not another year of having my two best friends separated from me at school that's throwing me off kilter—at least I don't realize until right now what it is. It's Adam's gregariousness, how easy it is for him to talk to people, how my peripheral vision has latched onto him and is watching everything he does no matter how I try to look away. He's so magnetic my eyes might disconnect from their sockets and attach themselves to him. Ever since I met him a button got pushed and I can't unpush it. I can't decide if I want to either, although I would like to feel less gripped in a vise.

A blond girl who looks like she might ride a longboard or something, septum piercing, perfect eyebrows, gives Adam a fist bump and then they talk. She pulls out a flask. She's very cool, apparently.

I don't have a flask.

"I guess I'll go eat worms," I say.

Turtle forces her way through the casually expensively well-dressed crowd and hands me a drink in a real glass, not even the red kind with the white rim. The drink is red though. The kind of red that kills people.

"Those guys over there are total wankers," Turtle says, nodding back to the boys hovering around the bar like crows. She sucks some spilled red drink from her own fingers. "Rich people, I swear."

"As opposed to extremely comfortable people?" Jack says.

This is the one thing I ever see them almost fight about. Turtle and I both live in suburbia a couple of blocks from each other. My house isn't as nice as hers but it is decent, three bedrooms and a yard with a tree and a swing hanging from its branches. Mom said that was the only thing they knew for sure they wanted. A tree from which they could hang a swing.

Jack is from Old Town where the buildings are crumbling and it's not a great idea to be out late at night by yourself. Jack's not comfortable. They have a popcorn ceiling and can hear their neighbors having sex when they're trying to go to sleep for school so they've been glad to be on summer break when the neighbor noises don't actually destroy their life. Also, while their parents do loan them a car sometimes, their parents suck in some fundamental ways. They're racists for one, and for another they don't even know about Turtle, and Jack says it should stay that way.

But this is a hell of a financial leap up from having a couple of TVs and a PC in the house. We're in the god realm now. No mere mortals exist in this sphere. None of these kids go to Owl Nook High. They probably think nothing of blowing $600 on a pair of sneakers, their parents schedule things like bikini waxes like it's normal, and they all drive new cars that are parked outside in the massive driveway that exists just for this house. I'm not saying this makes them better than us, but it definitely makes them different. I still can't totally believe Adam is one of them and I don't know what that means for me.

It's okay for a second and maybe perhaps my peripheral vision stops being so interested in the corner conversation, but then our banter trails off and it's only a few minutes before Turtle and Jack fall into each other's faces. I find myself at the bar, getting a refill. I slump into a corner, feeling warm down to my fingertips. I do not know why I don't drink more. Drinking is wonderful. First of all, it numbs feelings and feelings are gross. Second of all, my fingers are tingling and I'm a fan of that. I wrench myself out of the corner when I see Adam outside sitting by the pool on a sun chair.

I go to him, completely relieved he's left that girl inside.

"You're looking at the stars?" I say.

He looks me up and down. "You're wasted."

"Don't tell me I'm wasted."

"Sorry, you just seem like you are."

"Why do you want to talk about me being wasted?"

"I don't," he says.

"You having fun with Septum?" I grin even though inside I'm wincing.

"Septum?" He creases his brows and then understanding passes over him. "Cassie? I've known her since—"

"Never mind," I say. "I'm being stupid."

Then we both sit there for a while.

"*Sometimes as an antidote to fear of death, I eat the stars,*" he says finally.

"Okay."

"It's a poem written by a woman who died of cancer. Rebecca Elson. Non-Hodgkin lymphoma like my dad."

"Oh. I'm so sorry." What else can I say? I can only apologize over and over again.

"Are you okay, Blue?" he says. "Other than being buzzed? Did I do something?"

God, every time he says my name I lose my shit on the inside. Every time.

You have to learn to talk about your feelings.

For him. For Adam I will say things to try to describe something that is beyond words.

"You didn't message me." I stumble over my own tongue. "You didn't tell me you were going to be here."

"No." He looks totally shocked. "Was I supposed to?"

"And then you didn't talk to me when you saw me inside. It . . . hurt."

"Hurt? You didn't even look at me."

"Oh I was looking at you. I was looking at you all right."

Next to me, Adam freezes.

"And then you came out here and now you're talking about eating stars because while I'm thinking about you, you're dealing with something terrible and poetry comes easy to you. Adam," I say, "all I can do is think about you." My voice cracks and I push past everything that wants me to stop revealing myself. "You're the most attractive person I've ever met in my life. I don't know how I'm going to survive this. You're all I see when I look inside myself."

He holds my hand, runs the tip of his thumb over tender skin.

"Do you like me?" I say. I'm terrified this will mean a door closes instead of one opening. But I have to let out the person who lives inside. I have to let Inside Blue speak. "I know there's a lot happening, but I just need to know."

Adam holds my hand tighter, sits quiet for a moment.

"I don't even care if you don't," I lie. "I just can't keep going like this. And also, fuck your therapist."

Adam looks at me. Really looks at me. "You know what's funny?"

"What?"

"I'm here because I saw you were on the Snap Map, but then once I was here I didn't want you to feel like I was stalking you. I didn't know what to say or how to walk up to you. You make me not know what to say. And all the while, as I don't know what to say or how to be with you, my dad is dying. It's really happening now."

"Oh."

"My mom and my brothers and my little sister, plus my *tía*, have been at his bedside. He's real comfortable and everything but I think he's scared. I don't know what it means when the king of the jungle is scared."

"Adam." I lay my head on his shoulder. "I'm sorry I said mean things about your therapist. Really."

He snort sobs, then recovers. "I don't want you to feel sorry for me," he says.

"I don't," I say, even though I do.

"I don't want to kiss you because I'm scared of death, or because I'm scared of his death. I want to kiss you because I want to kiss you and because together we can eat the stars, but I don't think I'll be able to tell what I want or why until it's over," he says.

He thinks we can eat stars together. He thinks we can conquer the fear of death by being together. He also doesn't think we should be together until . . .

"Until he dies?"

Adam nods. "I'm being selfish. I want to keep you separate from that."

"Boys don't talk like this."

"You know a lot about boys?"

"I don't know shit."

"My dad looks like a shriveled up white finger," he says. Then

164

he lets out a laugh tear. "He's a brown dude, always had a big chest and got kinda pale in the winter but come summer he'd be outside for five minutes and his skin would be like, thank you, and he'd turn the right kind of brown again. Strong brown. But now it's August and he's so skinny and white and bald. He's like the ugliest baby ever."

He's crying next to me and it can be hard for guys to cry or to have people looking at them so I fold myself around his body and let him shake in my arms. My whole being exhales, like it's finally where it's supposed to be. I want him to be able to shed as many tears as he wants to and to know that I'll be here the whole time, and when he's done, and forever after.

The trees blow softly with summer and the sound rises and recedes just like on the beach. "That sound reminds me of you," I say into his back. "It sounds like how you feel."

My hand is still in his and he squeezes it and I'll do anything to freeze time and have our hands touching like this. I stare at my red Converse next to his killer kicks and think how he's a miracle and this is a miracle too.

Right now in the year of our lord two thousand thirty many things are true: Adam's dad is alive. My parents are together at home and there are two cars in the driveway and a wrecked RV my dad keeps saying he's going to fix up so we can drive it around the country whenever we feel like it. The worst my parents do is smoke joints out back after they think I'm asleep so herbal stink creeps through my window on nights when I leave it open to cool off, and lately they fight more than usual but things are basically good.

Life is happening and everyone is still whole and the music

beats on from inside and Adam and I are in this pocket, so invisible to the rest of the world it doesn't dare try to find us.

The vortex appears in front of me, an opalescent rainbow. I know what it is by now. This memory is over. I have to let go of Adam's hand and I don't want to. I want him to come with me.

"You'll see him again. Jump," Dr. Sweet's disembodied voice commands. "Jump."

vii

I fall into Arturo Mendoza's funeral, standing next to Gran. She's radiant if a little sweaty, her nails are done, and her hair's blown out. She looks *gorgeous*.

Even though she isn't Catholic or anything, Gran makes the sign of the cross twice, once as we pass the Lady of Guadalupe statue in the courtyard and again when we stumble over the threshold into the actual church. We don't stay inside for long though. The church is enormous, packed to capacity, and there's no place for us to sit. Kids too big for laps are sitting on parents' knees, others are making room for the elderly, shifting around.

I want to leave.

I want to leave so bad I'm gritting my teeth.

"He's not even going to know we're here," I say. "Look how many people there are. Even if he does know he's not going to care right now."

"We can find a spot outside where we can see into the service. They're going to leave the doors open so the people in the courtyard can still hear. It'll be fine. God willing there will be some shade for an old lady." She pulls a black lace fan out of her bag and then another one with red roses on it. She hands me the one with the roses.

"I'm not using this," I say.

"Oh I see, you're too good for my fan?"

"No, I just want to go home."

"Don't be such a pussy," she says.

I want to tell her she shouldn't swear like that in church but I don't think anyone heard her anyway and my throat's so dry I don't think I can speak. I haven't heard from Adam in a week even though I've been sending him texts every few hours. I was having Gran time at the aquarium when Adam let me know his dad had passed away. That's the last I heard from him. He said he'd be in touch when everything calmed down.

I'm down to sending him emojis, hearts mostly although I still feel weird about red ones. They all have meanings and none of them are quite right.

Which color heart means I will love you forever no matter what?

Which one means you're so precious you'll be in my life until I take my last breath?

You scare the shit out of me.

I'm sorry your heart is broken and your dad is dead.

I'll be here when it's all over.

And I am a pussy about stuff like this. I don't want to see a person in a casket and I don't know any of these people so being a witness to their personal tragedy doesn't seem right.

I don't like to see people in scraped knee kind of pain, never mind people trying to hold themselves together when everything is coming apart.

It's not that I don't feel anything.

I feel people fraying and I don't know how to hold them together when they're dissolving so all I can do is take them in through my veins. Then I don't know how to get them out of me and I carry their particles until I get blood poisoning and have to take a few days away from human beings altogether.

The service is called to order. A priest says some things about Jesus. There's a mic but I still can't quite hear. People around me are either crying or peering into the church. Gran has found a nice spot under a plum tree and is looking around like she will shank anyone who tries to come near her area. I can't see anything over the ocean of people, so I just listen to the prayers, the talk of God having a place in heaven for Arturo, that God will look over his wife and his children, that Arturo is free now.

The talking finally stops. I hear a sound, clear notes on a guitar.

"That's his son playing," a woman says to the man she's with.

A new level of hush falls over the courtyard. Even the ants are listening.

I stand up on the adobe wall and use Gran's head for leverage so I can see over the crowd. She doesn't complain, just keeps on fanning herself.

There's Adam.

He looks so different than how I pictured him over the last weeks. He's not as robust, looks more reedy and delicate, less like an athlete and more like a boy who plays a mean guitar.

Except this guitar isn't mean. It's complex, notes hopping over each other, altogether making a divine sound. It's like it's crying, weeping for everything it's lost. A man onstage claps his hands together and after a minute he begins to wail a mourning song, stomping his foot in time. Adam slaps the side of the guitar and the man howls and makes yipping noises, finally reaching a crescendo before the song abruptly ends and the churchyard is filled with its substance and the sound of everyone holding their breath at once.

Gran hands me a Kleenex.

There are no eulogies. That was it. One perfect song from Adam to his dad.

"He's so talented," the woman next to me says. "Just like his father."

"That concludes our ceremony," the priest says. "You may now pay your respects to the family and join us for the burial procession, then close friends and family may go to the Sunset River Bed-and-Breakfast for the reception. Thank you all for being here on this difficult day."

"Okay," I say, blowing my nose. "We did it. Let's go."

Gran, who has just stood up, puts the hand with the fan on her hip. "Now you listen to me," she says. "Someday it will be your turn. You will be the one who has lost. And you will not want to do it alone."

"He's not alone." I indicate to Gran, in case she's gone totally blind in the last hour, the literal hordes of people around us.

"I'm not finished, little miss sassafras," she says. "You will want the person who is most special to your heart to be there with you. He may have family and family is great, but for him you're the special one."

I start to protest and she puts up her hand. "And if I'm wrong, which I'm not, which I know because I have a ping, you have lost nothing except an August afternoon." She pats me on the butt with the fan. "Now move your tush. We're going to be last in line and I only have half a protein bar in my purse. You know what happens when I get low blood sugar."

The paparazzi snap pictures on every side. They aren't allowed in the church with their cameras and they stand chest-to-chest with security. The wait feels like forever and I can't see anything except a lot of black around me, and some people I'm pretty sure are family, because they look a little like Adam and they have red and pink roses tucked into their hair, like bridesmaids would do.

There's a brief parting of the seas and Adam comes into view. His mom is leaning on him. She's not much taller than me, if even by an inch. I can't believe how pretty she is in person. I see his brothers, Miguel and Isaiah and Johnny, and his sister Zinnia. All of them look like they've been emptied out, haven't slept, and they have to stand here and shake hundreds of hands.

The closer I get to Adam the harder my heart beats, the more my upper lip sweats, the fainter I feel, like his grief has made him a stranger. I don't even know if he'll recognize me anymore, blinded as he is by his loss.

Gran keeps one hand at the base of my back.

"You be strong," she says. "You make me proud."

I shake hands with his mother.

"Thank you for coming," she says.

"Thank you for having me." To my own horror, I curtsy.

Inside Blue. *Uch.*

And then I reach Adam. His face is all tear-streaked and everything and there's this huge line of people behind me. Gran is telling Adam's mom how we're friends and we talk all the time and Adam's mom says, Oh, this is the one? This is the girl? I feel her watching me with curiosity.

"I'm sorry I came," I whisper, thinking how I'm going to kill Gran as soon as we're out of here. I'm thinking how she never listens to me and is so aggressive because she's from Brooklyn or whatever and she doesn't understand that things are different here, and then Adam sort of falls into me.

Or no.

He drapes over me.

I don't stumble back or anything. I'm against his chest and he pulls me in so tight and I hug him back really tight because I think that's what he needs, maybe the only thing he needs. I feel like a bird in his arms because he's so big and I'm so small. I feel like he could suffocate me and also like I can save him right here and now. I know we aren't supposed to love people because we can save them, because that's codependent or something, but sometimes it just works out that way.

His mother nudges us out of the line so people can keep shaking hands and saying how sorry they are about Arturo.

"Who's that?" the little girl says very loudly. "Migue, who's Adam hugging like that?"

There are some titters.

Adam touches my cheek in a way I wouldn't like if anyone else did it, carefully, like it's a bird's egg. And then he pulls me back in, this time not so fiercely. This time like he just wants me to know I belong there. And we stand there like that with death all around us until Adam's mother tells us it's time to go to the cemetery and Gran asks about food after and tells her about the protein bar situation and then apologizes for talking about all that when it's such a hard day.

And Adam doesn't let go.

viii

It's getting heated.

It's *been* getting heated between us. It's like all those months of getting to know each other and everything that led up to Adam's dad's death and us finally becoming an actual couple planted fire in us we can't put out.

First there was kissing for hours and hours on end. *This is how we eat the stars,* he said. *This is how we conquer death.*

Then the shirts came off. We spent about a month like that, burning and burning.

Then pants got inched down and finally off. Couple showers have been had. By the winter holidays, we were living under blankets in his truck, stealing every second we could away from our families, just totally worshiping each other.

And now Adam Mendoza has his head between my legs.

Even with everything we've ever done to each other's bodies, I have no idea how I'm ever going to look at him again after this. What he's doing, how it's making me feel. Never did I ever

in my freakiest dreams even imagine this type of sensation was
an actual thing.

How do people go back to having normal conversations
without being all, *Hey so remember that time you had your head
between my legs*? How do they ever sit across from each other
and talk about what's for dinner or go for a normal walk in the
park when they have done all these things?

"Are you good?" he says.

"Uh-huh," I manage.

"Okay. Tell me if there's something I should be doing."

Adam is an overcommunicator. I'm discovering he is totally
unembarrassed by things he should be totally embarrassed by
and he likes to talk through everything.

And now I feel like I'm just hanging out for all to see while he
wants to have a conversation about it. No one's ever *looked* at
me before and I keep wanting to make sure he's not ogling or
anything. There's no need for him to learn every crease of me.
We're in my bedroom, true, and it's kind of dark and shadowy,
but I can't relax.

It's like I've forgotten something, someone I'm supposed to
be paying attention to.

"I don't know," I say. "This is the first time anyone's ... done
that."

"Gone down on you?"

"Adam. Stop saying words." I'm about to ignite.

He does stop saying words. I don't know what to do with myself and then I wish he would talk to me some more just so I
might have enough time to think, to get myself together. I don't
know how to take it. Heat is gathering, building, rising, and the

person I like the most on planet Earth is the one doing it, giving it to me. It's the best and most out-of-control thing I've ever felt, just like everything else I feel for Adam.

I let out a loud moan I can't keep in no matter how hard I try.

He puts a hand flat on my hip. "She'll hear," he says, before he goes back to what he was doing.

The dam is bursting, the itch I can't scratch is being scratched and I let it take me through the sparkling disco ball portal, away from Adam, and out of myself onto winged stars.

ix

We're at the farmers' market looking at some hats. The farmers' market has lettuce and carrots, jars of pickled cabbage, honey and fresh eggs, but there's also music and dancing, alpaca leggings, scarves, face painting, and watermelon juice. It's one of my favorite places to be on a summer morning. I used to come here with Mom and Dad to get the veggies for the week and the same woman still reads tarot cards from her little stand and waves at me when I go by.

Zinnia and Miguel are with us, running in circles. Zinnia is starting to look less like a little girl but still acts like one. She's caught in the middle of a transition that's awkward but also pulls at my heart. This is the last of childhood for her and mine already feels far behind me. I'm going into eleventh grade soon, and running around in circles with friends is something I haven't done in a long time.

I watch Zinnie from the mirror hung against the metal booth twirling in circles, arms held out like she has a partner, her hands curled, leaning outward at an impossible angle.

Who is she swinging with?

Whose hands is she holding?

I resume trying to decide if I can pull off a black velvet hat. They just came back in style and I like how they flop but I'm not sure my face is a hat face.

"That one looks good on you," Adam says, appearing behind me with a bag of peaches and a sack of piñon nuts.

Later, Gloria will make her pasta dish with chicken and pine nuts and sage, and it will be the best thing I've ever had to eat. It's become my favorite thing to sit with the loud and boisterous Mendoza family. My personal house has transformed into a sad place. My parents barely even talk to each other anymore. We haven't eaten dinner as a family in months.

Adam picks another, more of a bucket hat, and says, "Try this one."

It's taken almost a year of being together, but I can finally look at Adam without feeling like I'm in flames. The blinding want has turned into something tamer and deeper. I look at him and see every minute we've spent together from his father's funeral to the birthday dinner he planned for me this year. I see my life in him, even when we're doing something as trivial as walking around a farmers' market, but it doesn't make me feel like I need to writhe like it used to.

Zinnia bounds over. Miguel is over on the green hill now getting his face painted like a dragon.

"We want juices!" Zinnia says. "Can we have mint leaves in it?" She takes someone by the hand again and swings it, looking at me expectantly.

I squint to see who it is, this blank space. There have been too many blank spaces, things that should be one way and are another. I'm tired of not seeing but I'm also afraid. The sun shines down hot.

"I'll take this one," I say, deciding I like the bucket hat Adam suggested.

"I got it," Adam says, and he hands the woman ten dollars without fully taking his eyes from me. "You want to go get drinks? The weather's spicy today."

"Sure. You have everything you need for your mom's dinner?"

I'm talking to him but I'm also watching Zinnia carefully and a new thought is getting louder and louder.

Who is Zinnia holding hands with?

The ground quakes under me.

There are no earthquakes in New Mexico.

At least, there hasn't been an earthquake in New Mexico the whole time I've lived here.

I want to see what I cannot see. I want to see what I cannot see. I want to see what I cannot see.

When I look back at Zinnia I see the outline next to her taking full form until she is three-dimensional and in color. She has her arm entwined in Zinnia's and is maybe an inch taller. Her black hair is dyed purple at the ends and she's in denim shorts and a shirt that's white with strawberries on it.

"Hey!" I call to her, suddenly desperate to see her in her entirety.

She turns around, responding to the sound of my voice, and there's nothing where her face should be. I liquefy with terror.

"Do you see that?" I manage to ask Adam.

"What?" he answers. "#$%@^&."

It's garbled and I can't hear what he's saying.

The ground under me shakes again and a whine starts up in my ear.

Adam puts his arms around me, but I'm irritated and shrug him off.

"Why'd you do that?" Adam says.

"What?"

"Why'd you shrug me off like that?"

"I don't know. Something's wrong. The girl who's with Zinnie. I can't see her."

"Who? #$%@^&?"

"What are you saying?"

"What are *you* saying?" he demands.

Two women approach on stilts. They have flowing costumes in greens and blues and horns on their heads. They're throwing glitter and laughing in a tinkling way.

"We need money for them!" Zinnia runs at Adam. "Where's your wallet?"

Zinnia is obsessed with these ladies. She gives them money every week. Adam hands her a twenty and she runs up to the one in green silk. I follow behind, not wanting her to get lost in the fray. The other girl follows. I still can't see her face. I'm trying to act normal but it's not normal not to be able to see a person's face. Everything is crumbling and I can't get rid of that whine, which is only getting louder.

"Here!" Zinnia shouts up to the woman, who is hovering like a goddess above us. "Will you do a trick for me?"

The woman leans down so far I can't believe she's not toppling over.

"Larissa, come here! The girls want us to do a trick!" she calls to the woman with the copper hair, who's been slowly making her way up the corridor of stands.

There's a country band playing in the main square and it thumps even over here. Adam scoops Zinnia up onto his shoulders so she can see better. The other girl takes my hand and begins swinging it back and forth. I don't want to look at her and see her missing parts. This is beginning to feel like a bad dream.

Amor fati. Amor fati.

Love your fate.

The women on stilts set something at the end of a chain on fire and both begin twirling, watching the flames travel back and forth between them.

I'm holding onto this smaller hand.

"Adam," I call out. I can't see him anymore. And then everything and everyone disappears.

There is no Miguel, no Zinnia, no Adam.

There are no women twirling fire and no booths selling hats; no one is playing music. There is no sky overhead and no sun beating on my back.

There is only the Old Town square and a hand in mine that is attached to a girl with long black hair and purple at the ends and strawberries on her shirt, and her hand is warm and I still can't see her face. It's only a ripple.

"Adam," I call into the void. "Who is this? Who is holding my hand?"

I'm a blip, a nothing, not even close to five feet tall. I'm a millimeter if that.

Or I don't know what I am because I'm on a sheet of white, glaring as new snow on a sunny day. There's nothing here to give me any perspective.

"DR. SWEET," I call. "DR. SWEET! DR. SWEET, PLEASE HELP ME!"

"I'm here," she says. "I'm already here."

"There's someone I can't see," I say.

"Yes," Dr. Sweet says.

"This is the big thing? The thing no one would tell me?"

"Yes."

"It's the reason I did this? Had everything erased?"

"Yes."

"It's going to hurt to know?"

"Probably, yes."

"Is it going to make me want to die?"

"Maybe."

I sit. Fortunately there's ground in this place. I lie down. Down looks the same as up. It's all white. White forever. The movie screen in my mind is blank. It feels nice to lie down after all the moving around.

"Dr. Sweet," I say again.

"Yes."

"I want you to give it back to me."

"It?"

"The memory. The cutout."

The cutout. It.

"It?" she says again.

"Her," I amend. It's scary to say that word. *Her.*

"Her," Dr. Sweet says. "Ah."

"Give her back to me. The girl on the bus, downstairs, at the party, in the other room, at the market."

"She's already there. Understand?"

"Not really," I say.

"Breathe," Dr. Sweet says.

I do.

I inhale.

I exhale.

I inhale.

I exhale.

As I inhale this time, the white that's all around me climbs into my throat.

When I exhale the white is like a sheet coming off of a bed a little at a time. The white goes in my lungs. It fills up my stomach, replaces my intestines, overtakes my muscles and my bone.

I inhale one more time and the white is gone. I'm not standing in nothingness on an empty page. I'm back in the market. It's dark out, nighttime, the stars in this sky twinkling brighter than real ones.

I feel the squeezing again. I look down. There's a hand folded into mine. I want to fight it, to pull my hand away but I remember what Dr. Sweet said, that if I fight it . . . *her* . . . it will hurt even more. I'm my normal size now but we aren't in the normal world. We aren't in a memory. We're in between two panes of glass.

"Look over at me," a voice says.

There's an insistent tug at my hand.

"Don't look away."

I turn my head slowly, breathing in, breathing out.

I feel suddenly like if I do what the voice says I'll find an oozing corpse looking back at me, eyeballs dangling from a skull, rotting maggot-infested flesh. The hand in my hand is attached to a frothing monster, a psychopath with knives and a kill kit. This is not safe. This is the furthest thing from safe.

My eyes travel up the arm, the soft hairless skin, to the neck, and the head that nearly reaches my own. I can see her face now, her clear blue eyes, the face of my father, the face of my sister.

My. Sister.

"Do you remember me yet?" she says. "I can't breathe down there. Don't leave me."

The world shakes under my feet, an earthquake to pull all of reality apart and this time it does not come back together.

Oh God. God no.

"Blue. Blue," the little girl says. "You do. You remember me, don't you? I see it now. I feel you do."

She takes an inhale to match my own.

I sink to the sidewalk.

"I remember you," I say.

"Prove it. Who am I?" She's waiting for me, kindly, nudging me to say her name, to know who she is, to admit she exists.

Existed.

"Viola," I say. "You are Viola Rose."

Mysistermysistermysister.

"Yes," she says. "It feels very good to breathe."

x

Obviously, I don't love what's happening right now, but I'm more worried about V than anything else, the way she's picking her fingers raw at the edges so blood rises to the surface. We have been summoned from our rooms, V away from her new VR game, me away from a lazy afternoon nap after a late night with Adam.

I've known this was coming for a while, that our parents don't get along the way they used to. And so now the fact that we're gathered in the living room like a TV family, V and me sinking into the oversized pillows of our gray couch while the wind blows testily through the trees outside—it's not a surprise, but it is a disappointment.

V keeps looking at me like she expects me to do something, say something that's going to change this. For her, this is not just disappointing, it's terrifying.

"Everything's going to be okay," I tell her.

"No it's not," she says blandly, picking and picking. "It's never going to be okay again."

"Honey," Mom says. She looks small and uncomfortable in the dining chair across from us.

This is such a foreign configuration, an odd melding of worlds. When we're all together we're either adventuring or sitting around the kitchen table or all of us are stuffed onto the couch facing the TV. Circles that cut into our shared living space like this one spell trouble.

"The problem," Dad says, addressing us like we're disciples, "is that sometimes you think life's going to go one way and it doesn't. You imagine you'll be able to solve all these problems and you can't. You think you're going to stay together for your whole lives and one day you wake up and know that won't happen. Life is mysterious and unwieldy. You can't predict how you're going to feel."

"Did you get that wisdom off a coffee cup?" I say.

"And don't say 'can't' when you mean 'won't,'" V says. "You *won't* solve problems. You *won't* try to feel the way you're supposed to."

Mom's eyes well. They're pretending this is what they both want, but I can tell it's really what he wants from the way she leans back as he leans forward, from the way he keeps trying to explain himself. I wonder if he's hooked up with one of those rafting girls he works with, sturdy, beer-drinking, tan, young. Whether he has or not, the real problem as far as I can tell is that adulthood is a game where you try to ignore tiny cuts and then one day you wake up to find you've been hacked to pieces.

People get divorced all the time and it works out okay. Gloria's alone and coping without Arturo, raising all those kids with her sister's and Adam's help. Turtle's parents are also recently separated and are amenably co-parenting. My phone vibrates under my thigh where I've wedged it for the duration of this nightmare conversation. I'm supposed to be going to the Mountain for coffee with Turtle and Jack and Adam before we drive up to the sand dunes to camp for a couple days.

"Where are we going to live?" V asks.

Mom and Dad look at each other. They reek of guilt.

"You're going to sell the house?" I ask. I hadn't thought through it when I wondered if this was coming. When Turtle's parents got divorced they did something called Birdnesting, where she stayed in the house and they rotated weeks until finally Turtle's dad found a place to buy. She never had to pack up her room and leave.

"It's what we have," Mom says. "We have to. The house is the only thing we own that's worth anything. You know your dad and I have never earned more than we needed."

"Are we leaving Owl Nook?" I whine, hating the high-pitched squeal of it.

"No," Mom says. "At least I'm not. I want to be close to the mountains and Gran. But your dad—"

"There's time for all this," Dad says, shooting her a look. "We'll take it as it comes. For now, no one's going anywhere."

I've always appreciated that my parents are easygoing, that while other kids had routines and responsibilities they more or less left me alone to figure out what would work for me, but right now I want answers, deadlines, certainty, and Dad wants to be here now and see how it all unfolds or some shit. It's just an excuse. Sometimes I wonder if even though they wound up with this house, this marriage, these kids, my parents never really wanted to commit to anything, if they just fell into their lives without any thought.

"What happens when you sell the house?" V is only barely twelve, and she's toppled over the line from buoyant, giggling tween to cynical and grumpy pre-teen. It's like over the last couple of months as the fissure between our parents has become more apparent, she's had the joy sucked out of her bit by bit. The house at Tewa Court is always the thing we come back to, the gathering place.

"We thought maybe we'd stay at Gran's for a little while." Mom tries to smile but it's tight. "After the house sells."

V gets up from next to me and sits at Mom's feet. If we had to be divided I would belong to Dad and V would belong to Mom. We've never had to say before, but now lines will be drawn, allegiances will be formed, and it looks like while V will always stick with Mom, I may be left unmoored and bobbing around alone.

This time when the portal opens, a bright tunnel paved with roses, daisies, peonies, dahlias as big as my head, I'm grateful to step through, to let the whirling garden guide me, and I'm grateful when I land on a plane with V in my arms.

xi

Adam, V, and I shuffle off the jet bridge. V has been quiet the whole trip, only complaining once when she couldn't make the fan above her seat blow air onto her, and once when I wouldn't make room for her to use me as a pillow. I only fought her for a minute before I let her reposition me to her liking. She reeks of sadness lately and even her sour breath reminds me of everything she's lost in the last couple months.

The house on Tewa Court sold within a week of being on the market and we had to move in with Gran pretty much overnight. Most of our things were sold in an emergency yard sale and we put a few in the storage at Gran's apartment.

I felt the pain of it but not like V. I have Adam, Jack, Turtle. V has Zinnie but she's not old enough to make a family out of friends while all her stability is drawn and quartered.

Dad moved to Miami the second week in July because one

of his buddies had a job for him. He left me his truck and took a backpack and that was it. He packed quickly and with energy as he put everything in place while V and I watched him like he was a stranger. I don't think either of us wanted to come but he seduced us with promises of beaches and easy days. V cooed over Mom, making sure she was okay before she left. She was so worried about what Mom would do without us she got a stomachache. We both agreed to join Dad for a week on the condition that Adam could come with us too. He had to pay his own way but that was no problem. Gloria didn't like the imminent divorce or how V had been acting so sad lately or how my dad just went to Miami, so she opened her wallet wide.

Now we stumble through the airport only stopping to get cold drinks from a Hudson News refrigerator. V gulps down her Coke in two long pulls.

"I don't even like him anymore," she says as she tosses her bottle into a recycling container that says, RECYCLE, MIAMI/RECI-CLAR, MIAMI! in bright pink letters.

"Dad?" I say, even though I know that's who she means.

"Whatever," she answers as we step through the glass to the open part of the airport.

I can feel the judgment emanating from Adam. His stance is that as long as your parents love you and are doing the best they can, you take them as they are. At least they're on the planet and not dead. He doesn't say anything because he knows better. Every time he tries to defend Dad, V and I are on him like velociraptors.

We go straight to baggage claim, filing past old white women in big sunglasses with pink lipstick, and Black women with island accents, and brown women with wavy hair and gold necklaces. This place moves fast and loud and music pours out of storefronts as we seem to plod along at our New Mexico pace, slower and more heavy-footed than everyone around us.

I hardly recognize my own father as he speeds toward us. He's even tanner than when he's on the river. He's wearing a tank top and orange shorts, an outfit I never would have seen him in before, and he's lost about ten pounds. He leans in and gives both of us kisses on the cheeks and shakes Adam's hand, giving him a pat on the back. It's like he's trying to be faster than the situation, our potential rejection of him, whatever our feelings, what we might say if there was space and silence.

He charges to the car, talking all the while about seafood on the beach and his new apartment and how Miami has an energy unlike anything he's ever seen. These are summer people, he tells us, full of party and joy.

Can't we feel it?

The houses are green and blue and pink and the ocean pops up next to us as we drive into the city proper. The smell of it infiltrates Dad's king cab truck that's way nicer than the one he left behind in Owl Nook. Adam leans his head out the passenger seat window like a dog. He hasn't traveled anywhere since his dad died and I can see him absorbing the different air, closing his eyes to meet it and let it rush through him.

V looks out her own window, lips pursed, hands folded into fists in her lap. She doesn't respond to anything Dad says. She won't spare him a kind glance. Even I feel sorry for him. We park in an underground garage that is filled with electric BMWs and Mercedes, Teslas, and even a couple of Maseratis. You never see them in New Mexico, but especially not in bright yellow. The apartment Dad is living in is gorgeous. There's no other word for it. It's open and white from head to toe, with plush white leather couches and chairs and a kitchen with a marble island and a full set of stainless-steel pans hanging down. There's white carpeting too, and it's perfect, not a blemish to be seen anywhere.

Even Adam lets out a low whistle as he opens the living room doors that lead out onto a veranda overlooking the beach. He looks at me for confirmation but I refuse to give him the satisfaction of being impressed with a single thing about Dad's new life.

"It's Juan's."

Juan is Dad's buddy, a guy who liked to go rafting and spend a couple weeks in Owl Nook every year, so he and Dad got close. You would never know he was rich like that. I don't think even Dad did for a long time. He lives in Venezuela, apparently doesn't even use this place anymore, and needed someone to manage the apartment building that he owns. So here's Dad with a nice new truck, a chill job, and a beautiful apartment. No wife. No kids. How nice for him.

He leads us down the hall. "Blue, you can sleep in here. And V, you can be in here."

The rooms are even more sumptuous than the ones in Adam's house, which are earthy and dry. In here are vanities, soft towels, premium soaps and shampoos, and even two bathrobes hanging from the hooks in the bathroom.

"Sorry, bud," he says to Adam, "you can be on the couch. It folds out and is really comfortable."

"I'm sure," Adam says. "Thank you."

"I still feel like I'm in a hotel," Dad says, hovering in the doorway.

"Nicest one I've ever stayed in," I say, trying to keep the harshness at bay, my indignance that he's treating me like a baby, forcing me to sleep away from my only comfort.

He knows where V and I live now, that Gran's apartment is being held together by moxie and putty alone. And here he is acting high and mighty and moral. I wonder if he even gives Gran or Mom any money.

"I don't want to be here," V says, coming up behind Dad but keeping her distance. "Let's go to the beach."

I see the heartbreak pass over Dad, the dimming of defeat.

"Yeah, sure," he says. "Let's go."

We pass through a courtyard with a pool and some white metal tables and chairs, which Dad explains is a private restaurant for residents only. We can order anything we want from there, we just have to tell them his name. V gets another Coke and carries it out the gate, and Adam and I both get our reusable bottles filled. The beach is private of course, with white sand and perfect blue water. Dad tells us to be careful. The waves are stronger than they look and there's a riptide a little way out. He says we can come out here anytime. He says it's a perk. We sit on the beach and look out to where the sun is beginning to set.

"It's really nice to see you girls. You too, Adam."

"Yeah," Adam says. "It's nice to see you too. It seems good here."

"It is," Dad says gratefully.

V and I remain silent.

."Well." Dad scoots himself up to his feet. "You enjoy the water. I'm going to get us some Cuban sandwiches for dinner. They're the best you'll ever have, guaranteed."

"Okay," Adam says.

"A little on the nose don't you think?" I snap.

I am being such a bitch. It's like I can't stop myself. I look back, recognizing my father's slumped shoulders and more meandering gait. Things aren't going as he had hoped or planned.

"You two should stop hazing him," Adam says once he's out of sight.

"I'm not—"

"I hate him," V says, poking violently at the sand.

"Hate?" I repeat. I can't tell her that's not true because right now it is.

"He hasn't even asked about Mom."

I look over at Adam to see how he's going to respond, but everything gets muffled as the sand eats me up and spits me back out into the night.

TURTLE
What's happening down there?

ME
Nothing.

TURTLE
Boring. Aren't you supposed to be dancing the night away or something?

ME

So far we're just having awkward fam time.

TURTLE

V?

ME

Won't talk to Dad. Like, at all.

TURTLE

Ouch. Danny boy is a sensitive soul. How badly is he taking it?

ME

So far he's smiling through his tears.

TURTLE

So no clubbing?

ME

No.

TURTLE

Thong bikinis?

ME

NO!

TURTLE

How's the apartment?

ME

Extremely white.

TURTLE

Danny isn't going to last down there. He likes dirt.

ME

Not anymore. He looks . . . I don't know . . . not

totally happy but definitely healthier or something.

He has a youthful glow. It's nauseating.

TURTLE

Adam?

ME

He's siding with Dad on almost everything.

V is about to attack.

TURTLE

Feisty thing.

ME

She really is. Not like me.

TURTLE

Oh har har. You're funny.

ME

I can't believe we have to be here a whole week.

I don't know how we're going to make it.

TURTLE
You'll make it.

                                                    ME
                                        I'll do my best.

TURTLE
Hold on to Adam for support. It's what he's there for.

xii

We're on a dune at the beach, which is empty except for the three of us. Me, Adam, and V. It's early and kind of breezy still. Adam thought V would like this place because there's a little tide pool with sea anemone and small creatures, but V looks bored instead.

"Take me swimming." V sometimes acts like she's still ten, especially around Adam who brings out something flirty and petulant in her. She's adored him since that first run down the mountain. Sometimes I think she loves him even more than me.

"No swimming," I say. "There's a riptide."

"He said there was one spot, not that we couldn't swim at all. You're always so scared, Blue."

I think of flying down the mountain and I know what she says isn't true, but maybe she's talking about something else. Not being physically scared, being afraid of feelings or of life. Either way, it stings.

Also, when she acts like a little kid it makes me want to treat her more like a little kid. She's been like this since Mom and Dad split. It's like it's made her mean or something, like she's always at a deficit and the world owes her.

V flops onto the sand and eyes Adam until he gives me a pleading look and then goes to her. We're only three days into our trip and I'm sick of always being with V and Dad. It's like the walls are caving in. I'm only sixteen and I feel one million.

In the distance, V crouches down and runs her hands through the water, pushing her finger into the sea anemone and watching it retreat. I run up to where Adam is crouched down next to her, drape myself over his back.

"I'm going to get you alone," I say. "Tonight, come sneak into my bed."

"Your dad," he says. "I can't do that."

"Fuck my dad."

He gets that panicked look again.

"I don't mean it like that. I just mean I'm sick of thinking about other people all the time. It's not like we don't sleep together or something. He knows. I don't see what the big deal is."

I lean into his neck. He strokes my arms. A universe opens up in me.

He kisses my hand and rearranges himself. There's been tension between us lately, on multiple levels. I am more short-tempered than usual, I don't want to do what my parents say, I don't want to be on lockdown in Gran's little apartment, and I keep biking over to Tewa Court and staring at the house even though other people live there now.

I want to soften under his touch.

His touch softens me.

"It's not fair you got to have Adam here," V pouts. "I should have gotten to bring Zinnie."

This kid. She's literally never satisfied with anything. By seven in the morning she's painted, practiced her Spanish, and watched two shows. I can't keep up. Just a few more days.

"What if you let me dye your hair?" she says. "I can do a really good job. I've been watching videos. Or I could shave it for you. You could totally pull it off."

"In Dad's white apartment? Great idea. And I don't want to shave my head. I love my hair."

"What if I'm really careful?"

"No, V." My voice is rising. "What if you just calm down and give us some space? You're like a Chihuahua."

V gives me a dark look and stomps off toward the apartment, slamming the courtyard gate behind her.

"This isn't easy for her," Adam says. "And that was mean."

"Stop lecturing me," I say, settling beside him. "We're sisters. You don't get it."

"I have a sister."

"It's different," I insist.

"You should try being nice."

"You should try minding your own business. I'm serious."

There's only one woman on the beach with us. She has one of those mirror-looking things that helps tan her face. It's hot and sticky.

Adam thinks I'm being awful but he still guides me into the water where I wrap my legs around his waist and he dances me in slow circles through the sea until the fury in me quiets.

I'm getting out of the shower when I hear the argument start up. I've already done the outdoor shower to rid myself of sand and then dripped over the white carpeting into the marbled bathroom and into a second shower and V and Dad and Adam are in the living room putting out sandwiches and cold sodas for dinner. By the time we got back Dad had low music playing and was trying to set the scene for a good night together, but V went straight over to the TV and turned it on, letting the squeaking orchestra from her cartoon play over Dad's stereo.

I left, feeling a little bad for ditching Adam in my shitty family dynamics, but I had achieved my first peace since getting here or maybe in months and I didn't want to give it up. Last I saw, Adam had laid down a towel and then sat down next to V on the couch. So now, hearing the voices through the walls, recognizably my dad's and V's, I feel responsible for not being there to make everyone behave. If I hadn't seen Adam's family in action for so long I would be embarrassed, but for now I'm only alarmed.

I towel off and throw on a cotton beach cover-up. When I get into the living room, V turns on her heel.

"Dad is staying in Miami, did you know that?"

I had sort of assumed, actually, that his so-called summer job would be more permanent. I don't know if V hasn't been able to see how happy he is, but I'm shocked that she's shocked.

"Oh god." Dad sits down at the table, going limp everywhere but his forearms, which look like they're holding him in place. "This is not how I meant this to go. I wanted us to have a good night and for all of us to be together. It just slipped out."

I look at Adam, who's still on the couch, face betraying little emotion but watching as everything unfolds around him. He is the eye of the storm. I'll have to wait until later when we're alone for him to tell me his thoughts.

"He wants us to come live here," V says. "He wants us to leave Mom and Gran and Owl Nook and everything and come live with him."

Now I am stunned, frozen in place. I was expecting Dad to stay here but not for him to want us to come with him. I had assumed he would want to be free and unencumbered, not be a dad the way he was before.

"He doesn't even care about Mom at all." V is vibrating with rage, her hair in two purple braids. "Like I would ever leave her like you did."

Dad pounds a fist on the table and we all jump. He's been so agitated and nervous since we got here it's like we've gotten used to him trying to cater to us and now he's looking with real intensity at V.

"I'm sorry if things haven't turned out the way you wanted," he says. "They didn't turn out how I wanted either. I love your mom but we have stopped helping each other grow. There's no going back. We aren't getting back together, not ever."

V backs up and slumps onto the couch's arm, never taking her eyes from him.

"I think Miami is a better place to grow up and have oppor- tunities," he says. "There's a meth problem in Owl Nook and nothing to do. You have to have money now, to live well there. We don't need that. I can't get that for you there."

V snorts. I just stand there, water dripping down the front of my cover-up.

"You know why else I can't be in Owl Nook anymore? Be- cause the river's drying up and the climate is wrecking the snowfall. I have barely any jobs there anymore. I'm not a nurse like Gran or a contractor like your mom. I have no skills." He looks around. "But I have this. I have Juan's apartment and a private beach and a truck and money. I can handle some hurricanes every now and then. This is the first time I'm not living paycheck to paycheck in my whole adult life, that I don't have to take handouts from your grandpa to support my own family. It didn't work out between your mom and me and I'm sorry about that. I know you don't like it. But I can give you girls something good down here. Your mom can work from anywhere. There's no reason she can't come live here too, start fresh. This place is alive."

"Mom will never move here. She likes snow and cold," I say.

"There's air-conditioning," he says lamely.

"You know what I mean. She's not going to leave Owl Nook and you know it. If we left her you'd be taking away the only things holding her together. She hasn't been doing great lately."

Judging from the way he freezes he probably doesn't know. I bet she never talks to him on the phone unless she's her strongest self. She's not her strongest self very often lately.

"I don't mean to hurt her again. I want you girls to have every opportunity. That's all."

"Like Blue would leave Adam anyway," V mumbles.

I have never thought about that. Adam and I haven't discussed it at all. He graduated from his hybrid school without much fanfare and I'm going into my junior year now. I don't know what would happen if we moved.

"I get it," Dad says. "I don't want to mess with your scene."

The pause in conversation is so desperate I almost scream.

Adam gets up, goes over to the table, sits down, and takes a bite of a sandwich. "This is really good," he says.

Bless him. Bless every step he takes in this world.

Families are so intimate and raw. Even though Adam and I know each other like we do, I feel like now is when we really step over the line into *actually* knowing each other. First it was his dad and now it's my family falling apart. When you see the ugliness, that's when you really know you're in it.

Adam takes another bite. "Mmmm," he says.

V smiles for the first time in days. "You're such a dork, Adam." She saunters over to the table and takes the seat next to him. "Will *you* let me dye your hair?"

"You want to give my mama a heart attack?" he says. Then, "Sure, V. Do what you want."

Dad gives me one long, sad stare. I know what he's trying to say with it. *I'm sorry. I wish things were different. Can you forgive me for having a better life here? Do you still love me?* I retreat without letting him off the hook. I want to keep him on it, wriggling like a worm.

I walk down the hall, through the white veil, then up through the mattress onto the bed the next day.

I come out on top of the white blanket in the white room in the white Miami apartment with Adam, and my stomach goes into convulsions.

Adam's next to me but he's frozen in space. This memory hasn't started yet. All my bones hurt and I am between the memory and the now. I remember I'm in Dr. Sweet's apartment in a bed with something attached to my head that's making me see all this.

I'd like to be done now.

I'd like to wake up.

"Dr. Sweet!" I yell. "Hey! I don't want to see it again. Okay? I don't want to have to go through that."

"You weren't there the first time." The gentle voice quavers in the air around me.

"I was."

"Your body was there but your mind and heart left. You need this. You must be present to move through grief."

"I don't want to."

"We'll have to wait until you're ready."

"Are you saying I can't wake up until I do this?"

"That's right."

"Are you saying it metaphorically too?"

"That's right. Unless you do this you'll be asleep and unable to wake up to your life."

"I can't."

There's a tremulous sigh that shakes the ground under my feet.

"Try this," the voice says. "Where are you when it starts?"

"In bed with Adam. I mean not in, but on."

"Where's your father?"

"Miami. For some supplies for the building. New, more efficient light bulbs."

"Where is V?"

"She's . . . she's . . ."

"You can do this. Where is V?"

"She's in the living room."

"What happens?"

"She knocks on the door."

"Okay, let it take you. Remember, don't fight."

"Fighting makes it hurt worse."

"That's right. Fighting makes it hurt worse."

xiii

Adam and I are in the midst of a heated conversation when V knocks on the door.

"What?" I snap.

Adam gives me the look he gives when he thinks I'm being too harsh.

"I was going to see if you wanted to go to the beach," V says.

"No," I say. "Please go away."

Adam is already irritated with me and now he moves away from me. "We'll come in a few minutes, okay, V? Just wait for us. Go watch a show or something."

"I'm not five," she says, muffled through the door. "You can't just order me around."

"We'll be right out!" I yell. "Can we just get some fucking privacy for a second?"

I want so badly to get out of here and go back home. Miami doesn't suit my temperament. It's too humid and lively and filled with beautiful, tan people. I like my dry, thin air, and my semi-ornery mountain people.

Adam and I have been arguing. He's sitting on the bed with me, strumming on Dad's guitar, which is what he does when he doesn't want to talk. He just told me he was accepted to Berklee

College of Music and has decided not to go. I'm flushed with embarrassment and unexpected rage.

"This is totally fucked," I say, tucking my knees up to my chin. "You have to go."

"It's not because of you. It's for a lot of reasons. First of all, they took me because of my parents. I didn't even audition. My mom filmed me without me knowing and sent it in. You think this isn't because I'm Arturo Mendoza's kid?" He croaks bitterly. "Please."

"It's not because of my parents or because I won't be able to handle it if you leave?"

"No!" He lays the guitar down next to him. "You always think everything is about you."

The truth is the idea of Adam leaving me scares the ever-loving shit out of me, but there's also a part of me that wants him to go. We're going to have to separate eventually. Why not now when later is going to hurt so much worse? Might as well rip the Band-Aid off while I can still fathom life without him. The real truth is that sometimes I wish I'd never met Adam, that I'd never known he existed because then I wouldn't have to be scared all the time, counting down the minutes until he realized he wants a bigger, better life, girls dressed in mesh for festivals with beads hanging over their foreheads. Girls with big butts and boobs and money.

"It's not that," I say. "I don't want to be responsible for wrecking your life."

"You're not," he says. "I can't leave my mom right now. She's doing all this alone. And I know that's what she wants for me but I want to be here for her a little while longer. And if I'm here for you too, then how is that a bad thing?"

"I don't know. What if we're strangling each other, keeping each other from meeting other people or doing other things?"

He looks like I've punched him in the face. "Strangling? Is that how you feel?"

"No—"

"What other things? What *other people*?"

I stare ahead miserably, will myself into a smaller ball, will myself to disappear. I'm so tired of feeling.

"Maybe you're right," he says. "Maybe we're doomed and I thought we were forever."

He quietly leaves the room. I'm in tears right away, my face spouting water so my cheeks are sheeted and wet within seconds. Once I can pull myself together, I go into the living room to finish the conversation, but it's empty, the ceiling fan spinning redundantly, devoid of purpose since the room is already air-conditioned. I can smell traces of V, her raspberry shampoo and the vanilla milk body spray she loves so much that follows her around like a tail.

They went to the beach without me. Those fuckers.

That's what I think.

I splash water on my face and grab the gate card they didn't even bother to take, get a towel, and march out past the pool onto the hot sand. It feels like I'm standing in someone else's mouth. I think hateful thoughts again about this stupid place that has stolen my dad and made him whistle and wear orange denim shorts.

But then I see Adam and my throat drops into my toes. The world shimmers dangerously. He has V draped across his arm and is swimming ferociously toward the shore. She is limp, head hanging backward, neck tilted back and exposed like she's offering herself up to the sky. I quickly calculate how long V could have been out here alone. If she came down right after she knocked on the door she could have been down here maybe ten minutes total. I don't know how long I was crying in the bedroom but it couldn't have been more than a few.

I can't move my feet. The beach is totally deserted. Not even the lady with the mirror thing is here. All I can do is watch as Adam drags my sister to shore and force myself to go toward them instead of running away like I want to.

Like I wanted to then.

Like I want to now.

This is when I dissociate, turn into a zombie version of myself, when I see V with her lips already going blue, no color in her face, her fingertips an ugly purple. I drop to my knees and start performing CPR on her but my entire body is numb like I'm freezing when I'm also sweating, beads of water falling from my forehead onto hers. Adam says something to me about getting help and asks if I'm okay. I slap him away and go back to pumping and pumping.

The whole time I am thinking that this is not possible. This is not a possible thing. Water leaks out of V's mouth and I turn her to the side then back and I have no idea if I'm doing the right thing and try and try and try to wake her up and she doesn't and I just keep going at the rate they taught me in the class I took when I was a camp counselor last year. Camp Silver Eagle. That's what it was called.

Ah-ah-ah-ah stayin' alive stayin' alive

Ah-ah-ah-ah

I let the song play in my head over and over and pump. I don't get tired because I don't feel anything and by the time Adam returns with the guy from the building's fancy cafe and tells me the ambulance is on its way I know she's dead.

She will not be coming back.

I picture her stomping all the way out here and looking at the ocean like she's going to fight it. She scowls at it, throws her towel to the side, cursing me the whole time, and then she marches into the ocean. She wants to do battle with it and with me, to prove that she is tough enough to exist, to survive. She goes straight for the spot where Dad told us not to go, swims out there vowing to prove that we all underestimate her. She swims straight into a riptide, gets pulled under, flails and kicks but the riptide is too strong for her. She's carried away screaming when she reaches the surface, until she can't fight anymore.

Adam gets to her and tries to reclaim her from the ocean.

He brings her back to me, but it's too late and now I'm clinging to the last of the spirit in her body, willing her to stay connected to her skin and bones and organs and sinew and she is not listening to me. She is not following directions. She won't return.

By the time the ambulance comes, I am as gone as V.

My sister, is all I can think. Mysistermysistermysister.

My sister is dead.

"CAN I COME BACK OUT NOW?"

"No," Dr. Sweet says. "Almost but not yet."

"I ACCEPT IT. I ACCEPT WHAT HAPPENED."

"Not yet," she says.

I sink to the pretend ground.

"I CAN'T DO THIS. IT'S TOO MUCH."

"You can. All you have to do is walk through."

"WHEN WILL I GET TO THE END?"

"When you get to the end."

I stay in the white space for millennia.

I cry.

I pound my fists against a great nothing.

*I wish myself dead and alive again and I lose consciousness and
   I mourn.*

My little sister died on my watch

While I was watching someone else

Namely me

Worrying about stupid human tricks.

*I unwind and roll myself open and I'm in the water too and
   V swims to me*

Tucks herself onto my chest, body flush with mine

Hands clutching at the softest parts between ribs and hip bones.

*"You look good," she says, "but I could have done a better job
   with that hair."*

*We stay there like that until I've had enough to last me the jour-
   ney.*

I stand.

*The air whooshes toward me and I crouch like I do when I'm
   skiing because isn't that what life really is?*

Staying on your skis

*And sometimes it's cold and sometimes you get burned but it's
   always a thrill.*

A hole opens in the white. Behind it is the powerful darkness of the truth. Here are the hollow bones, the belly of the wave, the horizon out of sight. Amor fati. I don't know how you learn to love your fate and your own pain along with all your gifts, but I will.

I open my mouth wide, step through, and eat all the stars.

xiv

Most days when I wake up I wish I were dead.

It's been ten months since V died and I hardly remember any of it. I've slept most nights in her bedroom, wearing her body spray, clinging to her toy Oscar the Grouch, the last of her stuffies. I've gone to school sporadically, but sometimes I'm too tired. I'm so glad there's snow. There's this big aching part of myself that knows as soon as we round the horn into warmer weather, I'm going to feel even more and I don't think I have any more room, that I could be any more filled up than I already am.

There was a freak storm and Owl Nook is covered in snow and looking out the window of Gran's apartment I'm not surprised to find the twins from downstairs making snow angels while their parents look on. Mrs. Jenkins has her music going and this place has stopped feeling like someone else's house. This is where I live now.

Last week I saw Mom for the first time since she Canceled V and me.

She was shopping and I was with Adam at the center uptown where I never would have gone before, her hands tracing ghostly shadows over the racks of summer dresses, aspirationally displayed before their season. Her face looked simple, blank, a half smile plastered on and unmoving. Her nervousness was gone, the pain that had overtaken her physically and emotionally, keeping her in the fetal position staring at the TV, Gran constantly fluttering around her, offering her broth and Tylenol.

We became satellites of each other, never meeting eyes, hardly speaking. Every step I took was one V couldn't. And although my mother only told me once that it was my fault, accusation and blame lay thick between us.

So seeing her last week in that store, looking for a nice summer dress, I was jealous of her and her blankness, of her lack of knowledge, her simple blankness. Because I feel hollowed out by the repetition of days now, like everything that was in me right after V died was emptied and drained, but the memory of what was once there hasn't left me. It's there, like an emotional dental record, and will be used to identify my remains when I'm dead.

I made Adam follow my mother home to the apartment she got under the Spanish-style house in a cute part of town with vines climbing up its walls. I don't know why we felt like we had to hide, but we did, crouched down behind a tree, watching. She walked, untethered, wandering, never looking behind her. I told Adam my mom is a badass. She always told me she comes from a time of combat boots and punk music. She is not ethereal. She doesn't drift. Or at least she didn't before this.

Trailing her was the most alive I've felt in months.

Now, as I look out my bedroom window, I try to put Mom away, to tell myself this is what she wants. One of my therapists told me I'm not going to be able to take the hole away, but I can learn to find ways to live with it and to make peace with the things that aren't in my control. Ha. There is no peace.

I pry myself away from the window. Tonight is prom and I need to get my dress on. I know Adam wants us to have a normal night together. He wants me to wear something pretty and go have dinner with him. I go into the bathroom and look at myself. I'm greasy, my hair a nest on my head. V would never have allowed it. She was going to be a hair stylist and all she wanted was to dye my hair, to cut it. I couldn't even let her have that.

I find some scissors and chop chop it all up, leave it in a pile on the ground, then find the clipper in Pop-pop's old things and plug it in. I set it somewhere in the middle of the options, then I go to it, watching my hair fall off a strip at a time. I've always had long hair. This will be better, cleaner. I will look more like the me who lives inside now.

There you go, V. You can have it all.

I apply some black eyeliner, some red lipstick, and I'm ready to go. I'm sure Turtle and Jack are showering, doing hair, getting swanky, but I personally think this is going to be just fine for my stupid, shitty, run-down city prom.

I walk out into the living room and Gran, who has been watching TV, stands up with her lips parted like she wants to say something.

"What?" I say.

"Oh honey," she says, looking like she needs something to lean against, something to hold her steady.

"What?" I say again, this time with extra bite.

She holds up her phone. "I was going to take pictures."

"Well go ahead! Take one!"

She lifts the phone, hands trembling, and the flash goes off.

XV

I am at the party for Zinnia, on the portico outside Adam's that overlooks the pool. It's cold out but they have little heaters everywhere and people have their laps covered in sheepskin to keep warm.

There are maybe fifteen of us crowded around the table. Our empty plates are in front of us as Gloria's assistant, Enid, cleans off the table.

"You're not going to eat anything?" she says, close to my ear as she picks up my untouched plate.

Adam, who is next to me, rests his hand on my lap. I don't take it. I shake my head.

"Blue!" Zinnia calls. She has her birthday crown atop her head and is motioning for me to go be next to her. I know this is hard for her too, not having V here to celebrate with her.

I can't. It's been months since I could be with Zinnia without feeling like I am betraying V. And now Zinnie is turning thirteen and V never will.

Gloria is getting sick of my shit. I am also getting sick of my shit. She wants to be like, *My husband died, Adam lost his dad and we're bootstrapping it. Adam tried to save your sister when you were cruel and selfish. He has his own traumas. Why are you such a whiner?* She doesn't say that but I can hear it anyway, see it in her set mouth, her clacking nails. She gets up, making a little too much noise, and goes into the house.

"What's going on?" Adam says.

"Nothing."

We've hardly spoken since prom, since my bald head and too many drinks and flirtatious dancing with Marcus Cantu. I haven't been answering Adam's texts and they've slowed down recently, except it's Zinnie's birthday again and tradition is tradition. I have to be here for this.

Gloria comes out singing "Happy Birthday" and *Tía* joins in and pretty soon everyone at the table is belting out joy. It hurts my throat to see it. Gloria hands out lanterns, which we light on fire. Adam rubs my knee as the lanterns float into the air, into the night, flashing and sparkling and burning.

I picture how V would have looked, face illuminated and sparking with the possibility of magic, all her worries momentarily forgotten. For a moment I remember what happiness is. But then it flickers and is extinguished.

Thirty minutes later when the music has started and everyone is dancing to the music blaring from the house-wide speakers, I'm still staring upward, waiting for the lights to come back.

"Come dance!" Adam says, sweat glistening across his forehead. His *tía* has kept him moving for three songs without letting him sit down, all the while casting concerned glances my way.

I wish I could explain that all I want is to be alone with my sister, to get back what I had. This is an impossible thing, I know, but I still want it so badly I can almost taste it, can almost feel it.

Can we just get some fucking privacy for a second?

I take what's left of the cake, its careful fondant icing and delicate flowers and thin, stacked layers, and I carry it into the pool with me, fully clothed.

Somehow my twisted logic reasons that I'm taking it to V because V is underwater.

When Adam has retrieved me and covered me in a towel, and Gloria has given me some jeans and a sweater to borrow, she kneels down and tells me maybe Adam and I should take a break, maybe I should get some real help. She tells me, while Adam is making me tea, that I am ruining his life, that I have him in a chokehold. I already know that, so I just nod.

She's totally right. I'm a piece of shit and she should save her family while she can.

She calls Gran. They fight. When I get home Gran paces madly, yelling at the phone even though Gloria has hung up many minutes ago. She acts like she's defending me because that's what Gran does, but when she looks at me I can tell she thinks I should get help too. She reminds me I have that appointment with Dr. Vargas. Maybe with Mom and V and Dad gone, it's really just all too much for me.

Maybe, she says, unable to meet my eyes, it's time to hit the Cancel button.

xvi

We're in the auditorium, which is hosting Nationals this year for the show choir competition. Turtle and Jack have both been a mess. I've been backstage for an hour with them, trying to pick up the slack and do whatever they need me to. I never joined but I've been at so many of their rehearsals I'm accepted backstage, in the house, wherever I want to be.

There are kids practicing runs trilling up and down octaves, some of them not very well, and the other teams are trying to make themselves comfortable even though they're not on their home territory. Other coaches look judgily at our space and make comments about our green room, which Mr. Lovett is not super excited about. He personally rallied the town and raised the money for them to build this place eight years ago, which was basically a coup, so some lady from Albuquerque giving him attitude about it is not his favorite, especially when he's under stress.

Jack is in a tux with their sticks poking out of their back pocket and Turtle is somewhere, I don't know, having some sort of breakdown I'm sure because that's what she does before every performance. Then she pulls it together and does an amazing job, of course, but first she has to pee forty times and rip out half her hair.

I haven't been able to locate her in a while and I have her purse in my hand so I'm mostly watching this chaos unfold, trying to stay out of the way. A couple hours ago this was just a building and now it's a house of dreams or something. It's so filled up with things people want and all the feelings: dread, joy, everything. Me, I don't feel anything but pressure.

Pressure on my bones, against my muscle, on my head, in my stomach. That, and the constant feeling like something is going to unexpectedly drop out from under me, like no matter how I try there's no way I can predict what's coming around the horn for me, what bullshit event has my name on its roster.

Adam and I haven't spoken since Zinnie's birthday.

I told myself that was me hitting bottom. The bottom of a pool, that is (Ha ha, you're so funny, Blue).

I told myself the next day I would wake up, that I would be a new me. I would drink green tea and do some yoga, maybe go for a run and eat vegan and the feeling I've had for months now would be gone, because I'm stronger than it and because it's almost been an entire school year since V died and that means I should be getting myself together.

Everyone around me has been so tolerant, so patient, so forgiving. I owe them a better personality and a more resilient one and I was going to start the very next day. I could wake up and be that kind of person, one who glows and has goals and a self that doesn't torture them.

I would shower, maybe throw a little mousse on my bald head, and then I would go to a store, get some flowers, get something for Zinnie, and I would apologize for ruining her birthday. I would go talk to Gloria, face her. I would explain to her that I wasn't trying to keep Adam in a chokehold like she said. I'm not trying to keep him from living his life and being happy.

Adam would love me again. He wouldn't look at me like he was so tired every time I opened my mouth. Or didn't. Sex with him wouldn't be heavy and sad. We would be able to go up to the ski valley and walk along the tree line and hold hands and it would be beautiful like it was before.

We're summer love.

We're the couple everyone envies.

That's who we are, really.

All I have to do is find my way back there.

I can be whoever I want to be.

Liar, says the thing in me that's been talking ever since V died. *Such a dirty little liar all the time. Walking around like you don't have shit on your shoes. Shit in your heart. Tell them what really happened. Tell them how you told your sister to leave you alone before she did exactly that. They'll never be able to look at you again. No one will ever be able to forgive you if they know who you really are. They will see you and you will be ugly and rotting and the whole world will know it. There should be a prison for you. There should be nothing but locked doors for rotten girls like you.*

"Excuse me, Miss Blue, but have you seen the glitter machine?" Mr. Lovett says. "It's totally disappeared on me."

I'm so used to the voice now the things it says don't surprise me, but they do drag me under the surface so I can't hear what's above water sometimes.

I stand, still clutching Turtle's purse, trying to grasp what he just said to me, what I'm supposed to do right now, who I'm supposed to be. I paste on a smile. "No," I say carefully. "I haven't." Each word cuts my esophagus.

"That Mrs. Lorenzo probably hid it. She knows it's a huge part of the finale. I told them we should have this on neutral territory but unless we want to do it at Sun Stadium we have no choice in this state."

Help me, I want to say. I want to grab his hand and hold onto it and for him to pull me to the surface, but he doesn't even know I'm under anything so how can he? Anyway, he's super preoccupied with his search for the glitter machine.

I surface long enough to commiserate about Mrs. Lorenzo, ask him about Turtle, and then dip down again.

There's alone and then there's *alone.*

"Hey." Jack kneels down next to me and I worry about the

dust they could get on the knees of their tux pants but I can't move. "You okay?"

"Yes."

"Okay, because if you're not you can tell me."

"No." I'm falling falling sinking sinking. My voice is so far away I'm surprised Jack can hear me. I am under with V. "I couldn't find Turtle. I didn't know where else to go."

"Oh," Jack says, looking relieved. "Because of her stuff."

"Sure," I say. "Yeah. Because the guest teams took your lockers."

"Right," they say.

"Jack!" Mr. Lovett calls, rushing back our way with the glitter machine in hand. "Great. I was looking for you. The band is ready for sound check and we only have a fifteen-minute slot. Then I need you to help me with ten other things, which is only about five percent of the total things on my list. Yes? Great. Thanks."

"Yeah, coming," Jack says, hoisting themselves to their feet, looking down at me. "Why don't you go outside or go into the house and get the best seat. You don't have to hang out back here."

I hold up Turtle's purse.

Jack shakes their head. "No. I don't have anywhere to put it. You take it."

Now I'm a dot in a sea of red. I'm used to hanging out in the audience in the dark while they rehearse but this feels different. The stage and all the people coming and going reminds me that everything is a play and we're all acting out our lives. It isn't even really real. We come and go, easy peasy, bodies in, bodies out. We're flimsy and soft and breakable and the thing that holds us together is nothing but a bunch of particles and some water. We're really next to nothing.

Jack gets behind their kit and does some light tapping, checking to make sure everything sounds right. There's the kid on the guitar and the kid on the bass, and the kid on the trumpet. Turtle enters from stage left and scurries over to Jack, holding her gown up so it doesn't trail across the floor. I half stand to tell her about her purse when I realize no one actually gives a shit about the purse. She says something to Jack, who holds her by the shoulders and tells her something. A year ago I would have been a person Turtle could go to for emotional support in a tense moment. I would have been there for her and been able to manage doing more than this.

Because the truth is when my alarm woke me up the morning after the party, I couldn't move. I felt like I was a wrinkled piece of cotton under a hot iron. So I lay there hoping the feeling would leave and by the time it did I was long past the time for smoothies and yoga and the thought of green tea made me want to hurl and then Gran was puttering around and she wanted to have coffee and connect and I never got flowers or went over to Adam's or apologized to Zinnia and when I got done talking to Gran I had to go back to sleep and Adam didn't call me and so here I am.

Scuttling.

I'm driving Turtle's Jeep. I know this is a thing I should not do, that something is wrong with all of this, but I couldn't stay in there anymore and watch everyone being normal and swimming and doing grand somersaults out of the water while I was trapped underneath. I want to think about the road rolling under my tires. Turtle's tires. Whatever.

I love to drive.

I pass the hospital and the police station and the church and blast out going south where the road turns flat and long and the mountains are behind me and all those people and their songs and glitter machines are behind me too. This is raw, open road, the kind people like to ride on motorcycles. Maybe that's what I'll do. I'll get a motorcycle and take off, ride out into the great wide open. I won't be a crab anymore or if I am no one will know about it so no one will worry so no one will try to iron out my wrinkles and no one will mind if I lie flat on my back until I'm ready to get up again and get back on the bike.

I pull off the road, suddenly, surprising myself with one of those falling asleep jolts. But I'm not asleep. I'm at the Angel Wing Bridge.

Last time I was here it was for a ceremonial walk after Taylor Strong hucked himself off the edge. The whole community came together. There were medicine men and priests and activists and LGBTQ+ leaders and everyone was saying the same thing.

There's another way.

You don't have to do this.

This is a virus that is killing our young people. It's called suicide.

You could try EMDR, get your aura read, have a psychic therapy session, get your chakras balanced, sleep with the right crystal under your bed, take a cleansing bath naked in the moonlight, speak to a social worker, go to sacred hot springs, get blessed by a healer, use positive affirmations, take yourself to the hospital before you do anything rash, keep your loved ones around you, think of them, think of yourself, think of the life you could have if you just hold on. Think of your future spouse, future kids, future career. Think of the people you'd be leaving behind and how much you will hurt them if you do this. There will be more ceremonies and candlelight vigils and they will all have to learn how to go on without you.

Or, one man said, taking hold of the bullhorn. How about this?

Just. Erase. Everything.

Cancel it.

Back then I thought that was the stupidest thing I'd ever heard. Why would I ever want to erase anything about my life? There had been pain. I knew what life was. It was a series of events I couldn't control and some of them hurt and some of them didn't. In the end it was mostly good and you had to take some of the bad or you wouldn't realize how much of the good there really was.

Life was about balance.

I felt pretty confident about that, pretty happy I'd left V at home so she wouldn't have to hear about all this, so she could live without knowing people got so sad or shell-like that they would rather turn themselves into bloody human pancakes than live another day. Gran told me back when she was an EMT she was there when they pulled someone out of the can-yon. She said you couldn't tell his back from his front and if his boxer shorts hadn't still been on him she would never have known. That's how bad it would have to be to want to jump off this bridge.

It connects one side of a canyon to another, which seems pretty ironic to me. The thing that acts like a metal stitch over a wound in the rocks is the trapdoor human beings use as an exit ticket for planet earth. They are literally jumping into the hurt.

Sometimes there are tourists here, sometimes people selling jewelry. Now there's no one but me. The sun is beginning to set off in the distance. I can breathe up over the top for the first time in so long. The wind bites. It's waking me up and I'm not trapped underwater. I walk onto the bridge. I usually feel unsteady here because the ground is so far away under me and I don't like heights. Now I don't feel anything except like I want to be here, like it's the only place I can be right now. I walk past the emergency booths, the phones you can pick up if you're in despair and someone will come get you and keep you safe from yourself.

It's crazy how your own mind can attack you, like it's your worst enemy. The underwater voice isn't with me now. It's just me.

I breathe in and my lungs actually open and expand like they haven't been able to do in months.

I'm here.

I feel like I'm here.

I'm alive, and everything that's been looking like a paper cutout turns real again, fully three-dimensional, and I'm so grateful because I want to be here, I really do. I just don't know how to do it when all these things keep happening that are so out of my control all the time.

I lean over the edge of the bridge, look down at the river

and the trees down below. They're hardly visible from here, nothing but little dots.

Then I'm thinking about V and she's holding my hand even though she's too big to do it. She's practicing trimming my hair.

She's dancing with Adam.

She's watching movies with Zinnia. They throw popcorn at each other while Adam and I give them a hard time for blocking our view of the TV.

We're sitting in that special place that is only for sisters, having made a tent out of pastel sofa blankets in the living room. It's not the fort that's only for sisters, it's this other thing, this pocket of space we occupy. She's four and at school they've asked her what she wants to be when she grows up. She's been stymied by the question, so she's called a conference in her fort and has asked me for help. We've brought along a container of ice cream to help in the decision-making process.

"What if I don't grow up?" she asks me.

Even at seven I know what she's talking about. I remember so clearly the moment when I understood my parents would someday die. It was a resounding, echoing dread that seized my bones, followed by a visceral understanding that one day everything and everyone around me would be gone.

That, and the fact that Andy Guzman got run over in V's preschool parking lot by a dad who was on his phone and didn't see the kid behind him. We were standing right there and Mom couldn't get to covering V's eyes and sweeping her out of there before I saw V register what happened.

Me, I watched the whole thing. Never even blinked.

Since then, there are nights when V crawls into bed with me.

She holds one finger in her tiny hand and squeezes, sucking on her other thumb until she falls asleep. Sometimes she cries, but not a regular cry, the kind that would bring one of our parents to us, wondering what had happened. This is a low keen, the consequence of understanding her own mortality.

"You will grow up," I say. "You will."

"*If* I grow up, I want to make people pretty." She's obsessed with makeover shows. Watches them all the time.

"Don't say 'if.'" Her lack of confidence rattles me. "Say 'when.'"

She refuses staunchly and we finish the ice cream in silence.

What wouldn't I give to feel her small hand closing over mine.

She's going under and I can't stop it.

Her lungs are already full.

And this is what I go over and over in my mind. Did she know? Somehow did she know when she was four that she would never see fourteen? Is there fate? If there is, what is mine?

I hear the rumble of tires over the bridge and by the time I turn around and realize trouble has come for me, it's too late.

The cars are swinging into the parking lot.

I recognize Turtle's mom's Suburban as it pulls in first right next to the Jeep and then Adam's truck behind it, squeaking and rumbling.

"Oh shit," I whisper under my breath, clinging to metal.

The bridge is the only one who hears me.

Turtle's dress is picking up dirt the whole way to me.

Jack is not calm or cool and their face is contorted. They're yelling at me, I think, but I can't really hear over the rush of wind that's picked up inside my ear.

Turtle's mom is approaching slowly, keys in her hand. She's looking at me like she's never seen me before.

Adam is running.

I understand and step away from the edge.

They think I'm going to jump, that I came out here for that.

"I didn't," I start, but Turtle already has me by the arm. She's crying and yanking me toward the car.

When Adam gets to me Turtle moves out of the way. He doesn't touch me, stops short of that, but I see the relief. He thought he was going to find me at the bottom of the canyon, flattened maybe, in the water, caught on rocks. He thought he was too late. But instead of that, he doesn't know what he found. I see every single thing in his eyes, all over his face. There's been too much drama, too much death. I've lost it.

"You're alive," he says, and I'm not sure if it's because he's reassuring himself or because he's telling me and hopes I'll hear it. I hear it. I'm hearing it.

The only one who isn't in a total panic is Turtle's mom, Karen. She sees I fled and came here and I'm not in any real physical danger. I can tell by the way she clutches her brown sweater and fixes me with a stare. She doesn't feel sorry for me and she's not worried.

She's *pissed*.

"Do you know what you've done?" Karen says, each word measured. "Do you have *any* idea?"

I'm drawing a blank. What I've done? I went for a drive.

"Look," she says, pointing at my friends.

"Hey," Adam tries to interject.

"No, I've had enough. It's time to realize not everything is about you. Look at Turtle and Jack," Karen says, pointing with one perfectly manicured finger. "Really look at your supposed friends."

Jack is leaned against the car, slumped, looking at me dog-tired like they just ran a long race.

Turtle's dress is ruined. It's dirt-covered and her makeup looks garish in the light. Even her glitter looks tired and a little silly.

It hits me like forty fists in the belly all charging at once.

"You didn't even think about it?" Karen says, incredulous. "Are you telling me you didn't even *consider* what would happen if you stole Turtle's car and came out here while she's supposed to be having the crowning experience of her high school life? You think she would actually perform while thinking her best friend was out here possibly jumping off a bridge?" She lets out a hoarse, bitter laugh. "I knew it. This is just another grab for attention. Show choir had to use Jack's backup for drums. Turtle's solo was canceled, of course. They only had two numbers out of three so what do you think happens to the team? They could have won and it would have made this whole godawful year worth it."

I half-expect Turtle or Jack to stop her. I think Adam might step in. But no one does.

"If you need to go to the hospital and check yourself in, do it," Karen says. "If you need to get on medication, do it. But this is over, you understand me? Turtle's life does not revolve around you anymore. Her senior year has been ruined but I'm not going to stand for another minute of this. I'm not watching my beautiful daughter give you any more energy until and unless you start to help yourself, and even then there better be a serious change in your attitude."

Behind her the sky is on fire.

Karen turns her back on me and gets into the car, leaving me with Turtle and Jack and Adam, which is somehow worse.

"You okay?" Jack asks.

How many times have they asked me that question? One million?

"I don't know," I say. Then, "How did you find me?"

"Turtle's phone," Jack says. "When we couldn't find you before the show I checked. I thought you'd be in the parking lot or something. We saw the last place you had service and we knew."

"I'm really sorry about the show," I say.

"I know. It's been a hard year for everyone. We lost her too. And I don't know if it's just this or if you have something else going on, but you have to get some help."

They put out their hand and for a second I don't know what they want. But then I give them the keys I'm clutching.

Turtle doesn't say anything to me, but she remembers to hold up her dress as she climbs in. Both Karen's car and Turtle's Jeep roll out slowly as a funeral procession.

When everyone's gone and it's just Adam and me I say, "I'm going to call that guy. The memory one. I'm going to have it all taken out, tell him I'm keeping the appointment."

"No!"

"I have to."

Adam exhales.

"But not me though, right?" Adam says. "You won't erase me?"

"Stupid. I would never," I lie.

The sun dips behind the mountain and the sky goes a hazy gloaming blue.

Adam puts an arm around me and it's such a relief to have his skin touching mine I almost crumble. But I keep my back rigid. Because I keep fucking up in ways I can't seem to stop and I want him to touch me but I don't want him to be touched by me.

We sit on the hood of his truck as everything gets darker around us.

"It's the dome," he says, because the sky is so vast. Then, "I want to be there for you. I want to do what you did for me when my dad died. Except it happened to me too. I'm just trying to stay above water."

We both know what this means. It's not some abstract cliché. It's as real as real gets.

"Sometimes as an antidote to fear of death," I say.

"I eat the stars," he finishes.

"I'm sorry. So sorry for everything."

"Shit, Blue. You really went far today. Scared me half to death."

"Only half?" I say.

And we lie back against the window and I let myself be pulled onto his chest.

"You ever heard of susto?"

"No."

"It's when you get so scared or so hurt your body and soul get separated. I think that happened to you."

"How do you fix susto?" I ask, feeling myself hovering around us even now.

"I don't know," he says. "I wish I did."

A star floats toward us and opens into a vortex and sucks me in. I try to hold on to Adam but his T-shirt dissolves and becomes part of the sky and then I give in and let go and try to get ready for what comes next, but how can I do that when I don't know what it is? How can any of us be ready for anything? I crane my neck all the way back and do what Dr. Sweet said to do, what V did.

I surrender and career through a hurricane of glitter.

xvii

I fall out of the sky and onto V's bed. I'm not expecting this but I'm also not surprised and I don't have vertigo or anything. I feel mushy and pliable. On the other side of the door I hear Eunice barking so I get up and let her in. It's so nice to see her. It feels like it's been a very long time.

Adam is in the living room. I've asked him to let me be alone in here and he reluctantly agrees, pacing some before settling on the couch to watch a show.

Texts start coming when I turn my phone back on.

Turtle apologizes for crying while we were at the bridge.

Jack says they're sorry because they know I'm in a crisis and they should have been more supportive.

Zinnia tries to video chat twenty-three times.

And then Gran. Ten missed calls. Fifteen missed texts. Gran is trying to get her shift covered. Karen called her and told her what happened and can I please let her know I'm safe.

She shouldn't have gone to work this morning.

She knew there was something wrong.

She should always listen to her pings.

I text her back right away and tell her I'm fine, but she says she's coming home after she finishes her paperwork, so these are the last peaceful minutes I'm going to have for a while. I'm going to have a lot of explaining to do. Knowing Gran, we'll be up late into the night before she calms down.

V's room is covered in posters of boy bands. Her makeup is laid out across the vanity that used to be Mom's, pink lipsticks lined up across its flat, smooth surface. There's a picture of the three of us: Mom, Viola, and me. A comb with black and purple hair still caught in its teeth. Her clothes lined up and clean in a way they never would have been in real life, her shoes side by side as though she's going to come back at any instant and step into them.

I sit back against her satin pillow and sniff.

All this hopeful pink.

A needlepoint on the wall that says EVERY DAY IS A CLEAN SLATE.

My phone rings:

V IS CALLING . . .

V IS CALLING . . .

V IS CALLING . . .

I really have to change the contact information.

"Hi, Dad," I say.

He kept her phone after, and he keeps using it. I guess none of us are really okay.

Danny Owens doesn't speak to me for several seconds. "Blue?" he says. "You never answer."

"I'm answering now." I'm too tired to be edgy with him, so even though the words seem bladed, they're soft. I'm not even mad at him. I just want it all to stop.

"That's good, that's good."

My heart dips and lurches. I've missed the way his voice slides around words and how it's gravelly underneath like he's always at the edge of sleep.

He clears his throat. "Gina told me what happened at the bridge. She gave me an earful."

"I'm sure," I say, always surprised to hear Gran's real name like she's something other than my Gran sometimes. "Nothing really happened though. It all got blown out of proportion."

"So you weren't going out there to—"

"No!" I say. Then I pause, look around at all of Viola's things.

He takes a long, shaky breath. "I named you, you know that?"

I've heard this story before, but I want to hear it again. "You did?"

"Yeah." I hear the *chk chk* of his lighter, the quick inhale of smoke. "Your mom and Gina and Pop-pop wanted to name you Bianca. It was a good Italian name and you know them and all that Italian." I picture my dad, one foot hanging off a knee, the other one bouncing.

"Yeah," I say, closing my eyes.

"You were born in chaos."

"I was?" I let myself sink into the comfort of his familiar words, of a story with a beginning I can lean into and whose ending is assured.

"Yeah, there was this huge storm, one of those freak May things. When your mom started having contractions they were so fierce we didn't know if we'd make it to the hospital ten minutes away. I thought it would be one of those things where you'd be born in my truck and it'd be a story to tell if everything went okay. And then your mom was in labor for twenty-six hours. She pushed for so long we almost lost you. They were prepping the table for an emergency C-section and there you were at the last minute, a little purple and quiet, looking around like you knew exactly what everyone was up to, like you could see into all of us."

I imagine myself, barely a person, fighting to come here or maybe fighting not to, being born into a room full of people, looking around, checking it out.

He sucks in another breath of smoke. "I was so tired, the kind of tired that's hard to explain. I think it was different from your mom's. She was tired too, but all pumped up on her superhuman hormones. Me, I was still just a regular dude. Except I'd just witnessed something crazy. I never could go back to looking at your mom with anything but wonder after that. Anytime we'd argue, anything that ever came up, I'd just look at her and go, holy shit, she did twenty-six hours of hardcore pain to bring Blue to us. And it was worth it. You were worth it."

Tears hover at the edges of my lids. I try so hard to push them back but one slips over the edge and slides down my cheek.

"Anyway, I should have been in there with the two of you, but I felt like a prisoner. I needed to be outside, you know? My whole life had changed overnight and I was part of this miracle and I just needed to be away from everything, communing with the universe. Truth is, I didn't know if I could do it. I was a ski bum, man, a guy who liked to ride the rapids. I drank too much beer and cursed. I was excited to have a kid, but once you were born the weight of it settled on me and baby, it was not comfortable. So I went outside and I sat on this little adobe wall out there, and looked up. And there was this sky. It was this perfect blue that seemed to me to be every color at once. Blue like the ocean. Blue like my eyes. Blue like infinite peace."

My breath hitches. I hope he doesn't hear. I don't want him to stop.

"Well, you know the rest. I went back in there and told your mom your name was Blue. She let go of Bianca pretty easily."

"I would have made a really shitty Bianca."

"You would have been a color either way, but yeah, Blue suited you. It suits you now. Strong. Open."

That's how he thinks of me? I want to be that person. Clear of clouds.

"Anyway, you know you could come down here if you want. We could try to be a family again. I don't know how good I'll be at being a dad without your mom but I sure do love you, kid. I sure do want you with me."

I can't stop the tears now, all the ones I haven't been able to shed. They're all coming at once. I don't know if I cried the first time I heard this, because I don't know if I heard this at all.

My tears gather at my feet.

My father keeps talking.

My dog begins growling low in her throat.

My tears turn to waves, lifting the furniture.

I am under salty water.

I don't want to go back to this memory again.

I fight the water going into my lungs because I don't want to drown. I let go of the phone in my hand and it drifts away. Eunice barks underwater and it's muffled. Bubbles blow out of her mouth.

I'm holding my breath.

I'm holding my breath.

I'm holding my breath.

I remember what Dr. Sweet said. Resisting pain is what keeps it there. Fear loves tension.

I hope she's right.

I hope I can breathe underwater.

I let myself go, let my body go entirely limp. I know where I'm going and I already know what happened, so what does it matter if I look?

I inhale, and a whirlpool at my feet sucks me downward.

xviii

Mrs. Duran has her hands on her hips, her glasses perched on the tip of her nose. They look so precarious I'm surprised they stay on at all. Her mouth is pinched into a displeased O.

"Your parents don't have anything to say about this?" she says, staring at me levelly.

"My mom Canceled me. My dad's in Florida." I've already decided what I'm going to do and she's not going to talk me out of it, but she is sort of making me feel bad about it. I already gave her the letter, which she'll also have in electronic form, the one informing her of my decision and giving her some guidelines as to how to deal with me after. The paper version is currently sitting between us on one of her battered art tables. She put her glasses on to read it and they give her the look of a disapproving nun.

I expect her to say something nurturing and supportive but I can tell by the unmoved expression on her face that she's not going to.

"People die. Things happen. You go on. That's your job."

"But what if I can't?" I say. "What if I'm not strong enough?"

"So this is your solution?" She picks up the paper. "'If patient (Blue Owens) seems out of sorts, dizzy, or nauseated, you will need to provide ample water or a tall glass of orange juice. Do not mention any of the following subjects to patient (Blue Owens): Sister Viola Owens, Mother Sophia Owens, Boyfriend Adam Mendoza.'" She stops for a dramatic pause. "Are you serious? We used to drink orange juice to make the hallucinogens work faster. Now I'm wondering if maybe I never came down. This can't actually be happening."

I suppress an uptight giggle and make a mental note to tell Turtle that Mrs. Duran admitted to doing drugs before I have the memory expunged.

"I don't know what's happening to this world," she goes on. "You can't just delete things you don't like. You know what I heard? All the Richie Riches from uptown are doing it like they're getting their nails done. Bad meeting? Cancel. Date didn't like you? Cancel. It's like an abominable form of plastic surgery." She gazes upward. "I'm glad my Timmy didn't live to see this. He passed just in time."

Her Timmy was a nice man who was so tall he lurched and who left his house as little as possible unless they were going on a vacation or something.

"You know, in the eighties we wanted all the hard truths. We wanted to face things. It's been even more like that since the pandemic. People looking at history, racism, bigotry, what we've done to the planet, how we've treated each other, all the crazy false ideas we've had. We've rewritten everything. We've spent the last ten years trying to rebuild everything we broke with our lies. So this is a left turn I just wasn't expecting."

"Not everyone is as cool or as brave as you, Mrs. D."

"I've had plenty of crap happen in my life and I deal with it."

"Can I please just have my stuff?"

I don't mean to be rude, but this whole thing is grinding on me. I'd like to make high school one of the things I Cancel, maybe implant a lifetime of homeschool in its place. Mrs. Duran goes over to the portfolios lined up against the wall, sifts through them until she finds mine then slaps it down on the table, giving me a measured, almost dirty look the whole time.

"This is great work." She unzips it and opens to the first page, her hand rising to her heart and fluttering next to the gauzy pink of her blouse. Her eyes get watery. "What are you going to do with it?"

"It goes into some vault at Tabula Rasa." I try to say it like I don't care, but it's not true. This is the only way I've been able to express myself in the last months. Alone. There are the pictures of Turtle and Jack and me at the bridge that day, of Turtle on one of those SOS phones, of Jack and Turtle kissing with the canyon behind them.

"A vault?" Mrs. Duran says, shaking her head. "You're going to put this in a vault? That is not how art works. That is not what it's for."

There are pictures of Zinnia's small hands that remind me so much of V's, of rushing water, of Adam while he's sleeping, of the two of us, legs so entwined they look like branches. I used gold leaf on some of the pictures and underexposed them. Everything is in shadows with glimpses of light. It's my whole last year in symbols. It's everything I haven't been able to say out loud and all my missing pieces. I want to scream when I look at them, to hurl them across the room. I want them to go away as much as I want them to take away every bad thing that's happened to me.

Mrs. Duran is going on and on. She's picked up the letter again and is going through it point by point, ripping it to shreds.

Patient should turn over anything that might cause a memory. This is less dangerous than dissonance that may arise from it being missing.

Patient should be directed to lie down if at any time he/she/ they will not accept the explanation provided.

If patient persists in showing symptoms of difficulty a nap is advised as rest is required for assimilation.

"This is like what they used to do to women when they got upset about something. Doctors would call them hysterical and prescribe the rest cure. Have you heard of it? Of all the inane things to do . . ."

Me, I'm listening, sort of, but mostly I'm watching the gold leaf turn back to liquid and roll to the center of the page. I'm watching the gold flatten itself and open wider and wider. I'm watching it invite me in, drip by drip.

xix

I ride my bike up the hill. It's an almost impossible one to climb but I love the burning in my thighs and the pain in my lungs. It feels deserved. And I know after all this, whether he says yes or no or whatever, I'll have the ride down, legs loose and off the hook.

I push the buttons on the front gate and it swings open.

I walk my bike past the pool and the vegetable garden and the flower garden and the tennis courts, all the way up the driveway to his house. I feel as small now as I did the first time he brought me here. I limped into his arms in this part of the driveway and kissed him and it felt so good my feet tried to shrivel into themselves because I couldn't handle the solar flare that went off inside me.

Tenth grade seems like so long ago.

I can see him reading on the porch while he's half watching his brothers play, wearing that Gorillaz T-shirt we got at the reunion concert and a pair of shorts we bought from Target. That's one of the many things I love about him. He's a rich boy who couldn't give a damn about the name stamped across the bottom of his shoe.

I could write a poem about it, an infinite ode to him.

Adam's brothers are playing outside, and Johnny and Isaiah both run over to me and fling their arms around me. Johnny steps back because even though he's known me for two years now, he's still shy. Poor kid always has snot coming down his nose from allergies this time of year and there's a part of me that wants to run into the house right now and grab him a tissue from the entryway credenza where there's always a box waiting. But part of me also knows the inside of Adam's house is suddenly off-limits to me. I don't know what Gloria would do if I went in there now, but I do know she wouldn't hug me and drag me to the couch to tell her everything like she used to.

She always has a bowl of mints on the coffee table and she always smells like Prada la Femme, and her lips are always red red red and she used to hug me so hard I thought my entire rib cage would succumb and crack all at once. And I never liked anything so much as that. I want to hold on to every bit of it but I'll have to let it go if I want to get it back. She'll forgive me in time.

"Can you play hide-and-seek, Blue?" Isaiah asks, nearly jumping with eagerness. He looks like a mini-Adam and has the childlike version of his enthusiasm too, his unusual earnestness.

Johnny, who's eight now, watches me hopefully, and it just about kills me because of how much he chills out when he's playing. Miguel screams joyfully and hops through the bushes, the boys shooting water at each other with giant plastic machine guns.

"I can't play." I give them each a hug, insides lurching. "I just came to talk to Adam for a minute."

"Zinnie isn't here," Isaiah says. "She's going to be mad if you leave before she gets back."

"Zinnie's always mad about everything," I say.

Soon she'll be gone too. I obviously have to Cancel all of them. I can't forget Adam and remember his sister.

All things Adam must temporarily go.

The boys disappear into the sagebrush like they're already vanishing from my life, and I go over to Adam who's looking over the top of his book. His eyes are so clear I can see to the bottom of them even from here. Which means I can see all the hurt. I'm good at lying but Adam lacks talent in that department. He's a bone laid bare even when he tries to hide.

"What are you doing here?" he says.

"Came to say bye." I make my voice light and higher than usual, but I ache so badly I want to cry out to make it stop.

His hand is just right there.

He stands up tall, towering in front of me. If I lean forward my cheek will rest perfectly in his sternum.

"What's the point of saying goodbye?" he says now. "You won't remember anyway."

"Right." My heart gives a complicated thrum I'm surprised he can't hear. "So you won't do it?"

"My mom thinks you're crazy," he says, by way of answer.

I want to rail about how everyone has been overreacting but ever since I made this decision peace has settled over me like a blanket and it only gives a slight flutter now.

"But what do you think? I'm a little bit of a genius, right?" I'm trying to make light, but my body feels like it's begging.

"I don't know," he says. "I don't think you can just do that. I don't think it will work. What if you aren't attracted to me or something? What if we see each other and I don't recognize you? What if you're not my girl anymore?"

"What if I'm your girl but without the doom? Without the guilt and sadness," I say. "Wouldn't you want that? I would."

"Without V?"

Just the mention of her name sends an earthquake through me. "Yes. Without V."

"*Tsh*," he says. "I would never want that. What happened

happened, and that's what happened. How are you going to undo your own sister?"

"My mother did it. It will work if you let it."

"Yeah?" He shrugs. "I don't know."

"It'll be my birthday. At least meet me on the bus and say hello."

I knew this wasn't going to be an easy sell and as he sinks onto the porch stairs I can see how conflicted he is. He really hasn't decided yet.

"I can't go on like this," I say.

"You said you didn't go to the bridge for that."

"I didn't. Not that time."

He sucks his teeth.

"I've been calmer since we decided. I've been better. I can see clearly now," I say, trying to keep the pleading out of it. "Really. I've been chill."

"And if I don't do this crazy thing you want to do? If we never meet again?"

"It will still be better than this."

I don't let our bodies touch, but I sit down beside him. We watch the sunset together, each with our arms around our own knees. I love how the light lingers and clings, like it's reluctant to give over. Only another week of school left. Summer is coming again, and it's almost my birthday.

"Who the fuck is Dr. Vargas, anyway?" Adam says softly.

I don't answer. We'll just start fighting and I'm liking being with him and not arguing about anything. He turns to me like he can finally bear touching me now that this thing has really been decided and it's almost dark. Tomorrow I'll bathe, do a mask, clip and paint my nails. I'll lay out fresh clothes instead of wearing the sweats I've had on for a week. Until then I don't deserve shit. I'm still the person who killed my own sister, broke my mother's heart, who doesn't deserve this pure and beautiful love.

In front of us Isaiah perks up from a bush, visible under the porch light, and throws himself at Johnny.

We laugh and for a moment everything is back in its rightful place.

"See," Adam says, like the fact that we can still laugh together means we can handle all the rest of the absolute hellfire life has handed us in the last couple of years. "We didn't know what was going to happen."

"Adam."

"We didn't know. We did the best we could."

"Stop."

"It wasn't your fault. It wasn't anyone's fault."

"STOP!"

He flinches. "I loved her, and she was being a pain in the ass. Both things can be true at the same time. She didn't listen. Nothing was enough for her. She wouldn't even let us have one really important conversation."

"I was being awful."

"Sure. That happens sometimes when we're stressed out. It was too much for you to carry. There was too much going on. I don't know why you can't see that. V made her own choices, and no one was ever going to stop her."

I have to pull him out of the past. I don't want to be there anymore. I need to point him to the future where I can be the person he needs again.

"We can be happy."

"Happy." He repeats the word like he's tasting it for the first time. "Did you get rid of her stuff for your lobotomy or whatever?"

"We had to. And it's not a lobotomy. It's non-invasive."

"Yeah, says you."

The door squeaks open behind us. "Time to go inside," Gloria says, not a shred of warmth on her. She puts up her hand, silver bracelets jangling, like I shouldn't even try to talk to her right now, like she is not in the mood. "I need to pick your sister up from gymnastics." She's wiping her hands on a kitchen towel so violently I can just about feel them wringing my neck like I know she wishes she could.

"I know, Ma," he says, then glances back at her. "I'm coming."

When Gloria doesn't disappear, Adam sighs. "Ma. Go on."

Gloria makes a dissatisfied cluck and the screen door slaps shut. She mutters as she goes deeper into the house.

"See," I say, "it's all for the best. She'll have to love me again if I don't know who she is. I couldn't possibly be the same person who donated her cake to the pool."

"Too soon," Adam says. "You should have seen when she paid the pool-cleaning bill."

"Exactly my point."

I pull Adam to standing and he leans down and we kiss there as the first stars are just overhead. He opens his mouth and it's hot when he nips at my lips. It's not a sexy kiss so much as a communication. It's an apology, two years of a life spent together, going from almost babies to almost adults. It's eight seasons and so much pain. It's a plea and a thank-you and a lingering on something lost. It's every fight and every time we've made up and everything we discovered together. Most of all, it's a thank-you. His fingers dig into the base of my back and I edge out of his grasp before I melt again and lose all my will.

Adam grabs onto me, his fingertips brushing mine.

"You don't want to remember me?" He says this against my skin. "All of me. Everything we did?"

I'm dizzy with memory. Losing my virginity on that rock in the ski valley, how he padded it with blankets and was so afraid of hurting me, so careful. All our nights watching the sky together. His dad's death. When Isaiah broke his arm. All the times we held on to each other as we became less children and more of whatever we are now. I don't ever want to lose him, but forgetting him may be the only way.

And.

It's a moment of truth.

If he doesn't meet me on the bus, we're both free. He can go off to school or just start over with someone else and I'll never know. I'll never have to feel it.

"Meet me on the little blue bus," I answer. "At a quarter to eight, May nineteenth."

"You're breaking my heart, Blue."

When I can't stand to look at him anymore I shout into the yard, "Boys! Adam's taking you for ice cream when he goes into town to get Zinnie! Time to come inside."

"Hey!" he says. "That was a dirty trick."

Nothing calls to the hearts of young boys like the promise of sugar, and sure enough they slink out of the yard like shadows and charge up the steps scrabbling loudly at each other, swearing to fill up their water guns for round two. They stop short when they get to me, saying quiet goodbyes to me as they pass, seeming to grasp that something more serious is going on than usual. Even Johnny and Isaiah, who are truly going through that obnoxious twin phase where the most important things in their lives are online gaming and choice of cereals—even they take an extra minute to get indoors, eyes lingering between Adam and me like we're parents on the verge of a silent and unexpected divorce.

"Are you staying?" Miguel says.

"No. I'm sorry."

Miguel hurls himself into my arms. "Bye, Blue," he says and follows his brothers inside.

"I'll see you on my birthday?" I ask, with a savage surge of anxiety.

Adam traces my jaw one more time, then follows his brothers, letting the door close behind him.

Gloria swears from the hallway as she looks for her keys and I bolt to my bike, deerlike, running from the last person who might be able to convince me to stop this thing.

I write shakily on a piece of paper:

MEET ME ON THE LITTLE BLUE BUS
7:45 a.m. 5/19/32

I do my best to approximate Adam's handwriting even though I can't get it exactly right. I mostly just need it to not look like mine. Then I take the picture from last summer of me with Adam's siblings and I tape it to the back wall of my closet. Even if Adam doesn't show up and I never know who they are, I want this Remnant somewhere I'll eventually find it.

This is not part of the program.

This is something Dr. Sweet and Dr. Vargas would never approve of.

It's too dangerous messing with memories and what you know, what you don't. Forcing fate.

Too unwieldy.

They would tell me I'm playing with things I don't understand, that I'm like V wandering into unfamiliar water, tempting riptides.

But I've never wanted not to know Adam.

I only want to start over, and this is my insurance.

A vortex opens in front of me but this time when I step through it leads to a tunnel. There's dirt all around me. Vines grow from the ceiling or maybe those are root systems. Either way I have the feeling I'm not alone in here, that communication is happening that I can't see, a network of signals. I'm tired but it's not the kind of tired that makes me want to sleep, it's the kind that makes everything feel a little bit surreal. I guess that makes sense considering I'm in a tunnel in a part of my subconscious or something.

The side of the tunnel lights up in rectangles and I go to the first one. This is like when you go to the zoo and the reptiles are in cages in the wall, only it's not reptiles in there. It's me and my family.

I see myself at four years old. I'm holding a baby V. Mom and Dad are with me showing me how not to hurt her, how to be careful and make sure her head is supported. I take a few steps forward and there is V again, a little bigger, starting to walk, and I'm hovering around her making sure to catch her before she stumbles and falls to the ground.

I'm overjoyed to see me, her, our parents all whole again. And there's Gran! She's in one of her Sunday muumuus overseeing an art project. V is maybe three and I'm six and we're painting, getting more on the newspaper laid across the floor of Gran's apartment than on the canvas. Mine is of a rainbow and a house and sun. It's well done. V's is a chaos of color and yet it's somehow better than mine. Pop-pop comes up behind Gran and whispers something in her ear, then pats her on the butt. Little me doesn't notice. Big me, watching, grins even as my heart goes into the wood chipper.

I don't want to move on but I have no choice because the ground shifts under me like a conveyer belt and stops in front of the next window. It's V and me skiing and boarding, me shooting down the mountain while she follows in curving, graceful arcs. I can almost feel the frozen blast across my face.

It's V on the bus with her head leaned against my shoulder while I lean against Adam's.

V at the farmers' market, spinning in circles with Zinnia.

V giving the door at the apartment in Miami the finger then listening to Adam and me arguing. She goes to her phone, which is on the table in front of the TV. She pulls up my name and begins composing a text.

I hope you guys are okay.

She deletes it.

I'm going downstairs. I'll see you there.

She deletes again. It's getting louder from the bedroom. She pads softly to the door, grabbing her towel along the way and goes out into the hall. She gets a small smile on her face and I wonder why she's smiling. She goes through the court-yard, past the people at the pool and steps onto the hot sand. She's been carrying around this shroud of sadness and hurt that's turned her cantankerous but there's none of that now. She lays out her towel, takes a selfie and posts it, and then puts the phone down under her hat and walks to the water. She stretches her hands high above her head and yawns languor-ously before taking her first tentative steps in. She shivers with joy before diving in all the way.

She's swimming in the exact direction Dad told her not to go. She seems to be doing so deliberately as though called there. There's no hesitation and even when she's pulled under, it's si-lently as though she's falling into hands that are there waiting to catch her.

I touch the pane of glass separating me from this vision or whatever it is, because it's not a memory. Her hands come above the water, reaching for breath just as Adam comes out looking for her and then leaps into the panting sea.

The conveyor belt moves.

I am in a chair. People come in and out of the room. This, I know, is what came in the months after V's death. Therapists, shamans, EMDR specialists, aura readers, psychics . . . and all the while I sit and watch and retreat. I retreat from my own life until I'm not even a person anymore.

The conveyor belt inches forward.

I'm in a white room with my mother. She is crying so hard. It looks like she hasn't eaten or worn makeup or gotten properly dressed in months. I'm in a similar condition. Dr. Vargas and Dr. Sweet step into the room. Gran sits off to the side, hands clasped tightly across her lap. Dr. Sweet's lips flatten into a grim line that tells me she disagrees with the whole thing.

On the conveyor belt, my legs begin to feel weak.

"It's either this or we both die," my mother says. "We've already decided. I'd like to do it tonight."

My own mother wants to Cancel me. That's not the shocking part. That's something I already knew. The shock is that she wants to do it right away. Now. And when are we here? Everyone in the room is wearing a sweater and I have combat boots on my feet. Winter?

"She'll be fine," my mother says. "Her grandmother is going to take care of her. She won't even know I was here."

"You can't Cancel a mother," Dr. Sweet says. "We've never done that before."

Dr. Vargas leans back against the counter stuffed with

supplies: Q-tips, needles in sealed packages, vials of clear liquid with labels too small for me to read.

"We could try an implant," he says after a while.

"I died," Mom says. "Put that in there. That way she'll know she lost something and that she's grieving, but she won't know what."

"It could work," Dr. Vargas says, nodding slowly.

"And you?" Dr. Sweet asks my mother.

"Me? Oh, you can just Cancel me. I always wanted to be a mom, a wife. Not everyone wants that, but for me traveling the world with my babies on my back and my man by my side . . . that's all I ever wanted. So the fact that I'm a small independent contractor and have no one and nothing is reason enough to have a heavy heart. At least I won't know why. I won't know everything I did." She fingers the cuff of her sweater. "How long did you say it would take for the grief to leave my body?"

"Case like this," Dr. Sweet says. "A month? Maybe two?"

"It won't be instantaneous. But it will happen," Dr. Vargas assures her. He consults his papers. "Shall we do this tomorrow?"

Mom looks at me, but barely. "You can't do it today?"

How fast a person goes from being in the present, there in front of you, holding your hand or laughing at something stupid you said, and then a breath later there is silence where they used to be, a vacuum.

And then people start saying, right away, five minutes later: Oh, she was so special. Oh, she loved you so much. Even on the beach. She *was* your sister? She *was* a very special girl. She *was* such a spitfire, so intense, so rebellious.

Past tense.

Remember Me

Was.

She loved you so much.

She was such a good girl.

She was everyone's favorite.

And Adam. Trying to talk about it.

We didn't mean to.

She didn't listen.

She wasn't supposed to go to the beach alone.

She broke the rules.

She always broke the rules.

fifteen

When I wake up, I am screaming. Dr. Sweet holds my hand and I stop, but I am doubled into a fist and the tears that have already wet the sheets under my cheek keep flowing. I don't think they'll ever stop.

I remember everything. There are no more abstractions, no hazes, no half-conversations. I remember so hard I know what jumpsuit I wore on the first day of kindergarten and that at the end of the day when I took my pigtails down my whole head hurt. I remember every second of being V's sister, of being my mother's daughter, of being Gran's granddaughter. I remember every step I have ever taken on this earth, every hug I've given Turtle, every time I've leaned my head against Jack's shoulder, every time my dad smiled and that I realized he was a weak man and a kind one in the same breath. And I remember every blessed second with Adam.

I try to sit up.

"*Shhh*," Dr. Sweet whispers in my ear, leaning me back. "Breathe as you can."

I exhale.

"That's it," she says. "More just like that."

I remember smiles and sunshine and rainbows. I remember walking slow in tall grass, cool drinks in hot weather, clothes that make me feel like me, Gran yelling at the radio, Dad taking me fishing on a small boat, Adam and me walking through town pointing at crows. I remember him crying in my arms and me crying in his and his little black cat climbing the screen door and Gloria and her fancy Spanish floating lamps. Tea lights in the pool and Zinnia in my arms and Adam in my arms and Turtle in my arms too.

I remember that I am lucky to exist and that I should be screaming thank you for every single breath because thank you is the only right answer. Thank you for the ride. Thank you for every wacky turn of events that has led me right here. Thank you for my moments at the edge on the bridge, and for my mom's hard laugh, and for every sickening dip in the ride. Thank you for my friends, for my family.

Thank you for Dr. Sweet who gave me back my pain and gave me back myself.

My self.

This is *my* self.

No one else's.

No one else has the answer.

No one else even has the questions.

"I'm cold," I say to Dr. Sweet, my voice sandpaper and nails.

She leans back and exhales in her chair. Holds up fingers. "How many?"

"Three," I say.

She's sweating. "And who am I?"

"Dr. Erika Sweet," I say.

"All right then," she says.

She pushes a button and there's a sound like a plane landing and then letting its engine idle. I almost expect the speech they give you at the end of a flight like thank you for flying with Dr. Erika Sweet. Please be careful opening the overhead containers as all your memories and issues may have shifted during the flight.

Except it wasn't flying at five thousand feet. It was digging five thousand feet underground, picking up every piece of me that has ever been scattered and bringing it back home.

Pain and gratitude are exactly the same thing.

She takes my temperature. She takes my blood pressure.

"What day is it?" she asks.

"May twentieth."

"How old are you?"

"Seventeen."

"You okay?"

"Yeah," I say, answering honestly for the first time in forever. "I am. Thank you, Dr. Sweet," I say.

"He did it to me, you know. The doctor. I found out about it yesterday before you got here. He did the procedure on me. *Twice*. Well, twice I could find evidence of. Could be more. He convinced me. I listened to the stupid tapes. Because I want to change how things are done. Because I want to do more. But mostly because

I want to leave. I want to take the research I've done and what I've been able to develop and take it somewhere else. And then yesterday we had an argument right before you came. Something he said made me suspicious and I searched his office and found his notes about my procedure. Jeff is nothing if not fastidious about his record-keeping. Everything is an experiment to him. Even me."

I wait, still adjusting.

"I've been working with Jeff for ten years," she says. "How much of that time have I been wanting to leave? He knows about my research, but he doesn't know about Eve so he doesn't know to take her out of my memory." She looks around. "It's brilliant, really. He just sticks me into the Choose-Your-Own-Adventurator and *bam*, I forget all over again. Every time, I must go through the same thing, being so impressed by his intellect, being moved by his compassion for the pain of others, being seduced by his every word and all his passionate ideas. And he gets to be rewarded with the unmitigated adulation I give him every time I rediscover his brilliance. I went to Stanford, for God's sake! I can't go back there. I can't let him do it again. So thank you for proving to me that this can be done."

My eyes grow heavy, all my limbs still tingling with an adrenaline hangover.

She puts a blanket over me. "You're the cure for susto," I murmur, voice gritty as gravel.

And then I remember my mother. Because I can remember everything: the feel of her arms around me, the nearly purple rings around her eyes at the end. "Mom."

"Couple hours till sunrise," Dr. Sweet says. "Sleep, young one."

Before I leave to go back to Gran's, Dr. Sweet returns to me:

1. The shell on the hemp chain Adam and I got in Miami
2. The picture of us at Isaiah's confirmation
3. The picture of us by his pool
4. A picture of us at our first school dance
5. Concert tickets
6. Love letters Adam wrote me on actual paper with actual pen
7. The piece of my hoodie I gave him to wear as an armband when he competed in that snowboarding competition, like I was a maiden and he was a knight
8. All the pictures I took of V
9. A lock of purple hair
10. Everything I did in Mrs. Duran's class

It's a warm day, which is good because the ceremony is outside and if it were cold everyone would be miserable or we would have to move everything inside.

"Do you need me?" I ask Turtle.

She's about to go on and do her number with Kevin Orozco who seems to have finally figured out how to tolerate kissing her. She's in a red dress with a deep V-neck, and she did hair masks and used products and irons so her hair cascades in finger waves over her shoulders.

Jack's already behind the kit on the outdoor stage and I can feel them watching me. Considering what happened the last time I can't blame them so I try not to get defensive even on the inside. I have the whole summer to earn back their trust and try to salvage what I can before they leave. I don't feel so bad about what happened at the bridge anymore, like I did when I first woke up after Dr. Sweet. I get that I was having some sort of grief breakdown, but I also get that I wasn't thinking about anyone except myself and everyone around me got really tired. August will be here soon enough and they'll be gone. It's not that I want them to go, but I think we could all use a fresh start.

The right kind.

It still hurts whenever I think about V and I always want to push it away like some inside piece of me actually thinks I'll die if I have to remember her any more than I do. But then I remember about surrendering and I let myself scream or cry or whatever. I let it break me apart and I'm amazed every single time at how I come back together and am whole and am still alive and can breathe and everything.

Something is going to kill me, that's for sure, but it won't be grief.

Turtle, who has been holding a compact open while checking the edges of her red lips, snaps the mirror shut. "They could have at least given us access to the green room to get ready," she says. "Having to come here with our makeup completely done is so lame. And this harsh light . . ."

"Yeah," I say, smiling hard. "Totally."

She goes on nattering while I take a picture with my mind, get her into whatever place in my brain holds this memory and will myself to keep her there just like this, in her voluptuous diva state, in a red dress on a stage in the middle of a field in a small but growing city in New Mexico. I want to remember my best friend just as she is right now, complaining about the world with the best and greatest heart beating inside her chest.

She zips up her purse and hands it to me. "Hold on to this, would you?"

I do. "I'll be right here when you're done," I say. "I promise."

"Great," she says, already tromping off toward Jack, like it's nothing. But it is something.

I strap her purse across my torso and jump off the stage where Gran and Adam and his family are waiting for me. Zinnia slings an arm over my shoulder.

"I can't believe you're tall enough to do that," I say.

"It's 'cause you're really short," she says.

"I know, I know. You should hope to be short too. There's a lot of things that are easier."

"Not seeing over crowds," Adam says, looking smugly over all the heads around us.

Gloria leans over Gran's purse. "I know you have a protein bar and a fan in there, woman. Help a mommy out."

"I do. I also have some Kleenex."

"I don't cry," Gloria says, but she takes some anyway and starts fanning herself. "I hope it's a quiet summer, that's all I have to say."

"It'll be quiet, except when we go to Florida."

"I know, I know," Gloria says. She's still not my biggest fan, but I'll get there eventually. "Don't remind me."

A few days ago while Adam and I were having one of our never-ending conversations about everything we didn't talk about for almost a year, we decided it's time for me to go see my dad, like really see him for who he is without my mom and V and me. He said something about a girlfriend. Anyway, Adam wants to come. So do Gloria and Gran and all the kids. It'll be hard to be there at first, probably for all of us, but hard is okay.

"We don't need any more excitement," Gloria says. "Except maybe a little side trip to Disney World and some spa treatments. You know I love that mouse."

Just then the show choir comes jazzing through the crowd and they're basically immediately killing it. They've been really nice to me, all things considered, but I know they're still bristling from having their chance at Nationals destroyed by me. They are really giving it everything they've got. There's kicking and harmonizing and Jack is completely slaying and at the end when Turtle gets that kiss from Kevin, you could almost believe they're really into it, especially as a cloud of glitter showers over them.

Mr. Lovett looks absolutely thrilled from where he's standing off to the side, and I'm glad I didn't permanently ruin his year and he finally got to use his glitter machine.

That's when I remember I was in the belly of the wave, drowning along with my sister, and now I can see the horizon. But really, it was there all along.

Adam and I are in my dad's truck—correction, *my* truck. We're both looking over to my mother's apartment. I'm scared, terrified actually, but that's okay. I know V would want to be remembered, released, and kept close all at once.

"Are you sure you're ready for this?" Adam says.

"I think so."

"Because you could wait a little longer. You know, until you feel stronger or something."

"No," I say. "It's okay."

I roll up the windows and turn off the truck. I still almost can't believe this is real, that my mother is alive.

It explains so much.

The story was too neat. My dad didn't leave because of my mom's death. He left because they weren't working as a couple anymore. My mom didn't die in an avalanche. She just couldn't handle the reality of V's death any more than I could. That's why I couldn't remember the day Mom died. Real life isn't always as shiny as the memories we wish we had, but it is real and that's the important part.

Sometimes feelings get the better of us.

But I know now that they pass, or they pass and come back, but never the same as they were before.

"Some things are fate," I say.

"And what if I hadn't gotten on the little blue bus?"

"Then that would have been fate too."

I shiver. We were so close to missing each other. The slightest pull in another direction, more orange juice, less density, less listening to my own intuition, and Adam and I could have never met again. I might have never known about V, and I may never have discovered that my mom wasn't dead.

"I'm afraid," I say.

Adam and I have been speaking frankly a lot. At first it

seemed really strange saying things so bluntly but it's getting more natural to name emotions and then let them take me over and then let them go.

I'm sad.

I'm feeling shaky.

I'm so happy I'm with you.

I really like when you hold my hand.

"Why are you scared? About your mom? It'll be okay, I think," Adam says. "She'll be glad to see you."

"Or she won't."

"Yeah, or she won't," he says. "We'll do it a minute at a time."

"Okay."

"There she is."

Dr. Sweet has opened the door to my mother's house. She's been there all night. She gives us a wave and makes a motion for us to come in. Mom will already have remembered everything. She'll have remembered the good things too. Having V. Having me. She'll know every way she's made someone feel bad and every gift she's ever given. She'll be whole.

I want to give my mother what I have now. I can't take away the death, but I can help give her a new life.

Adam comes around and opens the door for me like he's not sure if I'll do it on my own. I put my foot down on the patch of grass outside the truck. He shuts the door.

Dr. Sweet motions to us again.

"You ready?" Adam says. He doesn't take my hand like he normally would and I don't offer it.

I take a few wobbly steps, my breath feeling like a balloon trying to pump itself up against a great resistance. I let it take me over. My lungs expand, and the anxiety that's been pulling at me all day settles and then disappears.

"Yeah," I say finally. "I'm ready."

Acknowledgments

To Sara Goodman: thanks for pushing me into new layers and encouraging the deep dive (and the climb). I adore working with you on the books of my heart. To Emily van Beek, always at the root, thank you for your continued friendship, support, and advocacy. I want to write you a song, something like: "You've always been there bay-bee / go ride your white horses," but I can't write songs. I'm also exceedingly grateful to Magda Manning and Anah Tillar for their authenticity reads with regard to the characters of Jack and Dr. Erika Sweet, respectively. At St. Martin's I owe a debt of gratitude to Alexis Neuville for the marketing, NaNá V. Stoelzle for the copyedits, Kerri Resnick for the cover of my dreams, Angelica Chong, Jennie Conway (editorial), Melanie Sanders (production editorial), Devan Norman (interior design), Brant Janeway (marketing), and Sarah Bonamino (publicity).

My kids, always my kids, Lilu and Bodhi. Not only are you impressive humans, you remind me daily that perfection is not a requirement for love—only patience, acceptance, and consciousness about how miraculous this crazy journey on planet earth is. I never go a day without recognizing my own beautiful fortune. My husband, Chris, for knowing me since we were the same age as Blue and Adam, and as a result understanding me in a singular way. I'm so grateful not to have to explain myself, and for every dinner made and early morning tolerated so I can pursue what lights me up.

My friends, both writing and not: SOMOS Young Writers Program and fellow board members; my moon women, Laine Overley, Sunny Moore, Johanna Debiase; my ladies of the perpetual text thread, Samantha Samoiel and Breanna Messerole; the father of my children and my forever friend, Cory Marchasin, and his partner, Lisa Stefany; my siblings; Taos Academy Charter School students and staff; NCW (hopefully by now we can see each other again); my parents; and Susan Marchasin and Carol Kublan, who together made an excellent jumping-off point for Gran. Special thanks and big gratitude to Danielle Paige, Marisa Reichardt, Jeff Zentner, Eliam Kraiem, David Arnold, Jasmine Warga, Sorboni Banerjee, Elana K. Arnold, Yvette Montoya, Elisa Romero, Jamie Lucero-Martinez, Mindy Laks, Kathleen Glasgow, Bonnie Pipkin, Sonya Feher, and John Biscello for the constant and lovely support and inspiration; Susan Mihalic for being my lone beta reader and for the excellent advice. I would also like to extend much gratitude to Oprah Winfrey's Super Soul podcast, which gave me the concept of the wave and the horizon, and most important introduced me to

Acknowledgments

Nietzsche's take on *amor fati,* which became such an important underlying thread.

Most and always, thank you to my readers, to the librarians, the educators, and everyone who ever gives one of my books a chance. All the love, always.